Jeremy is getting too attached to a woman of many mysteries.

Jeremy wiped a dish thoroughly and put it into the cabinet before he turned back and looked into April's eyes. "She says the DHR's willing to let Toni stay with the Potters, but not with you. She hinted that there would be trouble if we petitioned for you to be her guardian."

April lowered her eyes and, with studied diligence, resumed washing the dishes. "Did she say why?" she asked after a moment.

"She thinks you're too young and not stable enough."

Jeremy thought he detected a note of relief in April's voice. "Is that all?" Then she turned to face him. "Is that what you think?"

Almost automatically, Jeremy's arms went out to circle April's waist. "This is what I think," he said, then pulled her close and kissed her.

After a soft cry of surprise, April brought her hands out of the dishwater long enough to lay them lightly on Jeremy's shoulders. At first she answered his kiss with a light pressure, then she pulled away, picked up a dish towel, and dabbed at his shirt in the place where her hands had rested only a moment before.

"I'm afraid I got your shirt wet," she said.

"I don't mind." Jeremy caught April's hands in his and bent down to kiss her again. She did not resist, but when he would have deepened and prolonged the contact, she once more pulled away.

"Take me home now," April said levelly.

KAY CORNELIUS lives in Huntsville, Alabama. Mrs. Cornelius' talent for research and detail brings her stories to life. Each of her inspirational romances is an affirmation of "my own beliefs in the Lordship of Jesus Christ and the love of God that is the source of all human love."

Books by Kay Cornelius

Politically Correct

Kay Cornelius

Heartsong Presents

Dedicated with love to Teresa Reid Cornelius, tireless worker in the Alabama Department of Human Resources, devoted mother of my grandsons, Jake and Kyle, and steadfast wife to my son, Kevin Oldham Cornelius.

"Who can find a virtuous woman? for her price is far above rubies. . .Strength and honour are her clothing; and she shall rejoice in time to come. . .Her children arise up and call her blessed; her husband also, and he praiseth her." Proverbs 31:10, 25, 28

A note from the Author:
I love to hear from my readers! You may write to me at the following address: **Kay Cornelius**
Author Relations
P.O. Box 719
Uhrichsville, OH 44683

ISBN 1-57748-007-4

POLITICALLY CORRECT

Cover illustration by Chris Cocozza.

PRINTED IN THE U.S.A.

prologue

*"A wise man will hear, and will increase learning;
and a man of understanding shall attain unto wise
counsels."* Proverbs 1:5

In the lobby of a vintage building in the heart of
Washington, D.C., Jeremy Warren Winter took a deep,
steadying breath before he pushed the "Up" button on the
lone elevator. In a few moments he would enter the offices
of the Edwards Associates Company, where the entire
course of his future could be decided in a single interview.

Jeremy ran his finger around his collar, which suddenly
seemed too tight. His carefully chosen conservative, button-
down white shirt had returned from the laundry stiff with
too much starch, and he could almost feel his neck getting
redder by the moment. He glanced down at his tasteful blue-
and-gray striped tie and felt somewhat reassured. Jeremy
thought the tie blended well with his single-breasted navy
blue jacket and dove gray trousers. His obviously new,
wing-tip oxfords had started to pinch his broad feet, but
since he expected to sit down during his interview, he doubted that Mr. Guy Pettibone would notice his discomfort.

Guy Pettibone. Jeremy swallowed hard and wished in
vain that his interview with the man who had made, and
broken, so many politicians and would-be politicians was
safely concluded and that he was on his way back to
Alabama with Mr. Pettibone's stamp of approval. But in a
way, it would be a shame to waste the experience of meeting such a man for the first time. In the old days, political

careers had been decided in smoke-filled rooms. Now, however, image seemed to be the thing, and no one could beat Guy Pettibone when it came to making a candidate look worthy of being elected.

The elevator arrived, groaning and creaking, and Jeremy glanced at his watch. Assuming that the elevator would take no more than two minutes to bear him to the fifth floor, he should walk into the Edwards Associates office punctually at ten o'clock.

"Be on time. Don't get there too early and certainly don't be late," his Uncle Henry had advised him. Jeremy was aware that if ex-United States Senator Henry Marshall had not known Guy Pettibone for many years, the great political consultant would probably never have consented to see an unknown nobody like his nephew.

Well, Uncle Henry's influence might get me past the door, Jeremy thought, *but from there on it's up to me to make a good impression on Mr. Guy Pettibone.*

"I'll do it," he said aloud just as the wood-paneled elevator shuddered to a stop at the fifth floor and the doors opened with a jerk. Jeremy stepped out of the elevator directly into a reception area. He knew that the Edwards Associates public relations firm had many clients, but he had not expected it to occupy the entire floor.

"May I help you?" Mrs. Barnes, the silver-haired receptionist spoke to Jeremy with polite disdain, as if she could not imagine what business such a crass young man could possible have with a firm like Edwards Associates.

However, since Jeremy had already determined not to allow anything anyone said or did to affect him, he merely nodded and showed her Mr. Pettibone's letter and then announced, "Mr. Pettibone asked me to come at ten."

The woman glanced at the letter and then back at Jeremy.

Did she really look at him with more respect, or was it just his imagination? "I'll tell Mr. Pettibone you're here. You may wait over there."

Jeremy walked to the grouping of chairs she indicated and sat down, careful of the knife-sharp crease in his trousers. Uncle Henry had told him that Guy Pettibone was notorious for accepting or rejecting people on the basis of his first impressions, and Jeremy did not want to be dismissed out of hand because of a flaw in his appearance.

"Don't worry, Jeremy. Guy Pettibone wouldn't even agree to see you if he didn't think you have great potential," Henry Marshall had told him, but Jeremy knew that what he had put down in his resumé was probably far less important than the judgment Guy Pettibone would make when they met face to face.

Jeremy shifted in his chair and glanced covertly at his watch. *Of course he'll make me wait,* he thought without anger. Jeremy knew all about such strategies. In fact, Guy Pettibone might even be secretly observing him to see if he seemed uneasy.

I'm nervous enough, all right, Jeremy admitted, but one of his minor talents had always been an ability to disguise his true feelings. Most of the time Jeremy's expression looked thoughtful, even when he was not trying to appear that way. He seldom smiled (and therefore to great effect when he did), and only rarely did he lose his temper. Such traits might not be highly regarded in some quarters, but they could be quite valuable in a politician.

"Mr. Winter? I'm Mrs. Laura Tate, Mr. Pettibone's secretary. Come this way, please."

Startled, Jeremy looked up at an attractive young matron who had apparently emerged in silence from a hallway behind him.

I suppose that's part of the plan, too, Jeremy thought. He walked beside her down a long corridor that ended at a plain oak door.

Mrs. Tate knocked once, then opened the door and stuck her head inside. "Mr. Pettibone? Mr. Winter is here."

A muffled rumble came from the figure seated in a chair behind the desk. Guy Pettibone sat with his back turned to them, looking out a large window in which, framed in the distance, Jeremy recognized the dome of the United States Capitol Building. In spite of himself, he felt a thrill at the thought that one day, he could be a part of what went on in that very place.

"Go ahead." Not until the woman prompted him did Jeremy realize he still stood in the doorway. He started forward, and the figure in the chair turned, then rose and walked toward him.

He's even bigger than Uncle Henry said he was, Jeremy thought in awe. He knew that Guy Pettibone had been an all-American linebacker on a championship Texas college football team and then had played professional ball until injuries ended his career. However, Jeremy had not expected the man to dwarf his own height, or to be almost twice as wide. Since Guy Pettibone never gave interviews or allowed his picture to be taken, Jeremy had only his uncle's description to go by. Obviously, much had been left unsaid.

Guy Pettibone's clothing was not what Jeremy had anticipated, either. He wore a suit of some kind of almost iridescent material that changed from shades of brown to red and back again as the big man moved. On his oddly small feet he wore high-heeled, pointed-toed western boots fashioned of some strange kind of leather, into which his trousers were tucked, paratrooper style.

"Like these boots? They're ostrich skin. The little holes are where the feathers were," Guy Pettibone said when he saw Jeremy glance at them.

When Mr. Pettibone extended his hand to be shaken, Jeremy noted the gleam of a huge diamond ring on his pinkie finger. Careful to exert just the right amount of firm pressure, Jeremy returned the handshake and waited for Mr. Pettibone to speak again.

Guy Pettibone continued to look closely at Jeremy, and Jeremy looked back, determined to maintain eye contact with this imposing man. "You appear somewhat younger than I expected for thirty. Turn around, boy."

Boy? The man's thick, Texas accent made it a two-syllable word, but Jeremy sensed that it had not been intended as an insult. Dutifully, Jeremy made a low turn, as if publicly modeling his carefully chosen clothes.

"Sit down, sit down." Guy Pettibone waved expansively toward a pair of leather wing chairs in front of his desk. Jeremy sat on the edge of the nearer one, careful to keep his back straight.

"I presume you can talk, boy?" Mr. Pettibone said from the depths of his swiveling desk chair.

"Yes, sir, I can," Jeremy said clearly, "but I'm here today mostly to listen and learn."

Guy Pettibone's expression did not change. He grunted and picked up a riding crop that lay on top of his cluttered desk and leaned back, slapping it absently against the arm of his chair. "That's odd. I thought you'd come to ask me to help you prepare to run for a seat in the next Congressional elections. Or perhaps you have an agenda I don't know about?"

Jeremy sensed that he had made a mistake, but he would not compound it by forcing a lame apology. "No, sir. But I know you wouldn't be seeing me if you hadn't already pretty well decided that I was worth your time."

Guy Pettibone slapped the riding crop against his desk and guffawed. "Your uncle said you had a bit of sand in your craw. I like that. Now, tell me just what it is that you want from me, Mr. Winter."

Jeremy had prepared himself for this question, and he spoke without hesitation. "Mr. Pettibone, I was in high school when Uncle Henry went to the Senate. He got me a job as a page, and right then I knew I wanted a career in politics. I've done all I could to prepare myself for public service, but I know it takes more than the desire and a good education to get elected to office these days."

Guy Pettibone raised his eyebrows slightly. "Really? Just what else would you say it takes?"

Ignoring the slightly sarcastic note in Guy Pettibone's voice, Jeremy risked a slight smile. "Money, of course. . . lots of money. But to get that, the help and advice of a political consultant who knows the ins and outs of the system, someone who can guide a candidate through it. And of course, you're absolutely the best there is."

Guy Pettibone leaned back in his chair and crossed his arms over his ample chest. "Flattery doesn't impress me. I know who I am, but I'm still not sure about you." Then with narrowed eyes he leaned forward and pointed the riding crop directly at Jeremy. "You a drinking man? You ever do drugs?"

Jeremy had to resist the impulse to smile at the questions. "Neither. You could say I'm a world-class designated driver. I picked up a bad case of some kind of strange hepatitis overseas when I was a kid. As a result I can't ever drink, period. And I've always thought people who did drugs were stupid; my record there is absolutely clean."

"What about your general health?"

Jeremy shrugged. "No problems. I can't even remember the last time I was sick."

Guy Pettibone made another note on his pad. "How long has it been since you had a complete physical exam?"

"Two years, maybe. The doctor said he wished he had my heart rate and blood pressure."

"No doubt," Mr. Pettibone said dryly. "Now tell me about yourself, Mr. Winter."

Jeremy blinked, taken aback by the unexpected request. *I thought that's what I was doing,* he wanted to say. "It's all in my resumé."

Mr. Pettibone sighed and shook his head. "You majored in political science and went to law school and have since been working as one of fifty other nonpartners in a Birmingham firm. Big deal. So have dozens of others, maybe all brighter than you. What's different about Jeremy Warren Winter?"

Jeremy prided himself on his ability to think on his feet; he had even said so in his letter to Guy Pettibone. He took a deep breath, his mind already choosing his words. "My family's Alabama roots go way back. I'm not ashamed to say that my grandmother was a full-blooded Cherokee; I got my straight black hair and square face from her. My father's a retired army sergeant major who survived three different tours in Vietnam. Growing up on army bases all over this country and overseas, I learned how to get along with all kinds of people. I went to college on a scholarship, but I worked off and on during law school, which is why it took me so long to finish. Since then, my work in a large law firm convinced me that I don't want to do that the rest of my life. I'd like to get involved in politics as soon as possible."

Guy Pettibone glanced at Jeremy's resumé, then back at him. "I see that you plan to resign from the Birmingham firm and go to this town called Rockdale. Any particular reason?"

Jeremy nodded. "Several. For one thing, it's my home of record, and my grandmother left me property there. I'll be working with Randall Bell for the time being. The Rockdale Congressional District seat will be up for grabs if the incumbent retires at the end of the current term. . .and he's hinted he will. I'd like to run for it."

Guy Pettibone nodded and made a note on a blue legal pad. "Yes, I know Congressman Harrison. He's not a well man. What about your party affiliation? Will that be a problem?"

"I'm not sure what you mean."

"The way things are today, a party label can be a straightjacket. We like to see our candidates run in the party where we feel they have the best chance to win. Unless, of course, you aren't willing to change sides."

"I'm not really on either side. In fact, I've even been thinking I might run as an Independent."

Guy Pettibone grunted and made another note. "We'll have to do some research on that one." He leaned back in his chair and again pointed his riding crop at Jeremy. "Just how far are you willing to go to get elected, Mr. Winter?"

Jeremy had expected that he might be asked such a question, and he spoke almost automatically. "I won't do anything illegal or immoral, if that's what you mean."

"I never ask my clients to break the law, and if I ever find out you have, that'd be the end of our relationship. But I can advise you on what you need to do to be elected. If you can't promise to act on my advice, then I don't want you as my client."

"I'd want to know what it involves first," Jeremy said.

Guy Pettibone laughed. "No days like that, Mr. Winter. Either you trust me or you don't. I don't give free samples. If I'm willing to sign an unknown quantity like you as an Edwards Associates client, then you must be willing to let me guide you. Period. End of the discussion. Got it?"

He's good, Jeremy thought admiringly. Being accepted as Guy Pettibone's client would be a giant step toward realizing his ambitions; it was probably the single most important thing that could happen to his political career.

Jeremy nodded. "I understand. I'd have to be pretty crazy to ask for your help and not follow through on your advice."

"Or stupid." Mr. Pettibone opened a desk drawer and withdrew a sheaf of papers. He thumbed through them until he found what he searched for, then handed it across the desk to Jeremy. "Our standard contract," he explained as Jeremy scanned the brief document. "As you can see, we require a retainer on signing, then certain other payments from time to time. Either of us can cancel the agreement with due notice but there will be no refund of moneys already paid."

Jeremy looked across the desk at Guy Pettibone. "Will I owe you more money when I win?"

Guy Pettibone guffawed again. "You ought to, and that's a pure fact. However, I work for a flat fee, win, lose, or draw, and only on one race at a time. After you've been in the House of Representatives for a couple of terms, you might get a hankering to make a run for the Senate. If so, we'll negotiate again."

Mr. Pettibone's matter-of-fact assumption that he would be elected to the House made Jeremy's heart beat a little faster. He wet his lips and handed the contract back. "This looks fair to me. Where do I sign?"

"Hold it. . .we need a witness."

Mr. Pettibone spoke into his telephone and the woman who had brought Jeremy to the office soon entered the office.

"Mr. Winter will be joining us as a client, Mrs. Tate," he told her.

"How nice," she said politely. Jeremy wondered how many other times she had said the same words to other hopeful young men and women.

"I'm looking forward to it," Jeremy said, although he was not sure at this point exactly all that "it" might entail.

Mrs. Tate handed Jeremy two copies of the contract and showed him where to sign it. After Mr. Pettibone added his illegible scrawl, she signed as a witness and handed one copy to Jeremy. "Here you are, Mr. Winter. Stop by the receptionist's desk on the way out. Mrs. Barnes will take your check and give you a packet of general information."

"What kind of information?" Jeremy asked as Mrs. Tate left the room. "Is this when I get the secret handshake?"

Guy Pettibone ignored Jeremy's feeble attempt at humor. "More like our fax number and that sort of thing." He rose from his chair and stood before Jeremy, who felt dwarfed by comparison. "We have a lot of work to do and not very much time to do it in. It's a good thing you didn't wait any longer to come to me. Use this to take notes. I won't repeat what I'm about to say."

Surprised, Jeremy took the fresh blue legal pad that Guy Pettibone held out, then patted his pocket and realized he did not have a pen.

Seeing Jeremy's problem, Mr. Pettibone handed him a pen from the several in his own shirt pocket. "I'm about to tell you some things that will help you get elected, and the first is to carry a small notebook and a pen with you always, everywhere you go. When you meet people, write down their names or make some note about them on their business cards. File them promptly and consult them often."

Jeremy nodded. "I usually have several pens, but—"

"Let me do the talking," Mr. Pettibone interrupted. "As of five minutes ago, you're paying me to talk to you, not the other way around. Now, about your clothes."

Jeremy glanced down at his carefully selected outfit, then back up to see Mr. Pettibone shaking his head.

"That get-up might be fine in the big city, but it's all wrong for that district you aim to represent. In a few days I'll send you a memo about the look you need. Meanwhile, get yourself some shoes that fit."

Jeremy nodded, chagrined. "What else?"

Mr. Pettibone went back to the desk and picked up Jeremy's resumé. "You don't mention any church affiliation. You're not one of those New Age weirdos, are you?"

Jeremy almost smiled, then quickly thought better of it. "No, sir."

"Then you must find a church and join it as soon as possible."

Jeremy was not sure where Guy Pettibone was going with this suggestion. "Er. . .what sort of church?"

Mr. Pettibone shrugged and waved his hands vaguely in the air. "Oh, any church, as long as it has respected people of the community among its members. Mainstream is your best bet. You don't want to get identified with anything fringe or too trendy. Image, boy, image. It all has to do with the way the community sees you. Religion is in, politically speaking."

"Umm. . .all right." Jeremy made a note, then looked back at Mr. Pettibone, who had apparently noticed something else he did not like in his resumé.

"You're almost thirty years old and you're still single," Guy Pettibone said almost accusingly. "HYBs may get a certain number of women's votes, but in the end they lose a lot more."

"What's a hib?" asked Jeremy, thoroughly confused.

"HYB," Mr. Pettibone explained patiently. "Handsome Young Bachelor. . .HYB. But perhaps you're already engaged or seeing someone?"

Jeremy shook his head. "No, sir. To tell the truth, I've always thought that women were a distraction I didn't have the time nor money to afford."

Mr. Pettibone waved his hands and vigorously shook his head. "On the contrary. These days a successful candidate can't afford not to have an attractive wife. I suggest that you start looking around. I'm sure there must be any number of intelligent, good-looking women both willing and able to help you get elected."

Jeremy looked closely at Guy Pettibone, but the man seemed to be absolutely sincere. *He's telling me I should get married,* Jeremy thought with wonder. He made another note on the blue legal pad and looked warily toward his new mentor, almost afraid to hear what he might suggest next.

"Well, what about it? Will you take my advice?"

"I'll see what I can do." If Jeremy's voice lacked conviction, Mr. Pettibone did not seem to notice.

"Very good, Mr. Winter. By the way, I love your name. The minute I saw it I hoped we could work together. Are you known by Jeremy?"

"Yes. My mother wanted to call me Jere, but Dad said that sounded like a girl's name, so I've always been Jeremy."

"Good. It has a strong sound to it. And the Warren. . .a family name?"

"My mother was a Warren and there are still lots of them living around Rockdale."

"Excellent! You ought to work up a family tree, maybe even sponsor a family reunion. Besides being a good source of votes, family ties are big and getting bigger."

Jeremy's head had begun to feel light, as if he and reality were no longer in strict contact, but dutifully he made yet another note. "My family," he echoed.

"Your last name is absolutely made to order, you know," Guy Pettibone said.

Jeremy raised his eyebrows and waited to hear why. It did not take long.

Mr. Pettibone lifted both arms in the air and made punching gestures with his fists. "Win with Winter! Win, win, Winter! Winner Winter!"

He dropped his hands to his sides and grinned. "Couldn't ask for catchier political slogans than those, eh, Mr. Winter?"

"I suppose not." Jeremy's ears still rang from Mr. Pettibone's enthusiastic cheers, and warily he wondered what other surprises the political consultant might have in store for him.

Mr. Pettibone looked at his watch, then at Jeremy. "I'm sorry, but I have another appointment. If I think of other things to tell you, I'll call. Also, I need you to send regular progress reports. The details are in the material you'll get on your way out."

Jeremy rose and offered Mr. Pettibone his hand. "Thank you, sir. I really appreciate what you're doing for me."

"For us, Mr. Winter, for us. Tell that uncle of yours to come to see me sometime, you hear. Washington misses him."

"Yes, sir, I will."

A few minutes later, Jeremy took the heavy packet from the receptionist and shakily signed the check that officially made him Guy Pettibone's client. In the elevator he checked his watch, surprised to see that his entire stay at Edwards Associates had lasted less than half an hour.

So little time for so much to happen, Jeremy thought.

He walked from the dim lobby and blinked in the bright sunshine. Outwardly he might look the same, but inwardly Jeremy Warren Winter felt almost catastrophically altered.

Jeremy glanced at the words he had scribbled on the blue legal pad, the first commands for his new life as an aspiring politician.

> *Take notes (names, etc.)*
> *Get new clothes (as per Pettibone)*
> *Go to church (regular one)*
> *Get married (!)*
> *Make family tree (reunions?)*

Several large orders for anyone to consider, Jeremy reflected. But Guy Pettibone knew his business. And to get what he wanted, Jeremy would willingly make every effort to do as he had been told.

one

Jeremy Warren Winter drove toward Rockdale on a blustery March day that gave little assurance that warmer weather would ever arrive. As he left the highway and turned onto the narrow, two-lane road that would lead him to his new life, Jeremy thought of the changes that had taken place in the weeks since he had become Guy Pettibone's client.

From the way he dressed (loafers instead of wing-tips, more casual jackets and trousers) and wore his hair (longer in front, with part sweeping his forehead) to the car he now drove (a three-year-old, American-made sedan), Jeremy had followed his mentor's every suggestion.

"I rather like your new look," Jeremy's sister, Janice, had said when he stopped by her suburban Birmingham home on his way to Rockdale. She touched the unruly shock of hair above his right eyebrow and smiled. "There's just one thing: you'd better get yourself a stick."

"A stick?" Jeremy repeated.

Janice's dark brown eyes, so like her brother's, sparkled with amusement. "You'll need something to beat off the Rockdale women," she had explained. "I know how small towns operate. Once the word gets out that you're an eligible bachelor, you'll be fair game."

Jeremy's face warmed briefly at the thought. He had not told Janice about Guy Pettibone's admonition that he should get married before campaigning for political office, but he knew she would probably endorse the idea. When

Jeremy had turned thirty, Janice had frowned in exasperation when he arrived at his birthday celebration without a date. Jeremy had gone out with only a few young women during his time in Birmingham but none that he had cared for his sister to meet.

"You're not getting younger," she had reminded him. "Don't wait too long to start looking for a wife. All the good prospects will be taken."

"Maybe so, but I haven't yet seen anyone I want to spend the rest of my life with," Jeremy had truthfully replied.

"And at the rate you're going, you never will," Janice had said.

"Don't worry about it. The woman of my dreams could be waiting for me in Rockdale this very moment."

Jeremy had spoken lightly, and Janice had laughed with him. But now, as he came ever closer to Rockdale, Jeremy allowed himself to wonder if his frivolous statement might turn out to be true, after all. The whole idea of marrying for political convenience had been the most distasteful of the many suggestions that Guy Pettibone had made, and the only one about which Jeremy had serious reservations.

Mr. Pettibone can't make me marry against my will, Jeremy reminded himself.

If he happened to find someone he really wanted to marry by the time he announced for Wayne Harrison's seat, fine and good. If not, he doubted that Mr. Pettibone would withdraw his aid. After all, their contract had no "marriage clause" as a requirement for Edwards Asso-ciates to continue to represent him.

Jeremy nodded as if something had been settled, then realized that he had almost driven past the turnoff to Rockdale. The narrow, blacktop road wound some distance up a steep grade, then snaked down into the protected valley where the town lay.

"Rockdale may be in the middle of nowhere, but it's still the prettiest place this side of heaven," Jeremy's mother had often said of her home town.

She was right about that, Jeremy thought. Even now, without the lush green vegetation that was yet to come, the stark landscape held its own beauty and symmetry.

Skeletal trees interspersed with pines and cedars, and a tangle of dormant vines lined both sides of the narrow road, effectively screening the few houses from view. Only an occasional mailbox and the logging roads that intersected the highway gave any hint of civilization. Jeremy passed the spot where a well-remembered, everlasting spring erupted from a cleft in the rocky hillside, only to disappear mysteriously into a hole in the ground a few feet away. He had been only five or six years old when his grandmother had first awed him with the sight. "It's like magic," Jeremy had told her.

His grandmother had nodded and spoken seriously. "In a way, it is, Jeremy. This spring comes from so deep in the earth that it never stops running, even in the driest weather. The Cherokee say it is a gift from God."

It's no wonder my Cherokee ancestors didn't want to leave this place, Jeremy thought. According to his grandmother, in 1838, when the Cherokee were ordered to leave the land they had considered to be theirs from time immemorial, her people had instead gone into hiding in the remote reaches of the forested mountains of northeastern Alabama. Fearing they would also be forced to relocate to that far-off land now known as Oklahoma, several successive generations of the family had stayed on in the deep woods.

When logging finally forced them out, the family had

settled in Rockdale, where Jeremy's grandmother, Rebecca, grew up to marry a prosperous white man named Warren, who had made a fortune from timber. However, Jeremy's grandmother never forgot the old Cherokee stories and, through the years, whenever Jeremy and Janice visited her, Rebecca Warren always repeated the tales to them.

Jeremy sighed, remembering the last time he had seen his grandmother, when he had come to Rockdale one cold November to see his mother laid to rest in the family cemetery on Warren Mountain. He had been fifteen then, living in California where his father was stationed. Jeremy's grandmother had held him tightly when he said good-bye, and he had promised he would return to Rockdale as usual in the summer.

But instead, Jeremy's uncle had arranged for him to be a page, and he had gone to Washington. After that, Jeremy worked every summer to help pay his own way. His father soon remarried, and Adele, his new wife, wanted no part of the place where Jeremy's mother had lived.

Jeremy's eyes blurred as he recalled his next trip to Rockdale, a few years later, when he returned to bury his grandmother.

"What do you plan to do with Mrs. Warren's property?" Randall Bell had asked Jeremy then. As Rebecca Warren's lawyer, Mr. Bell knew that she had willed most of her money to Janice and all of her property to Jeremy. "You could get a good price for it, I suspect," he had added when Jeremy made no immediate reply.

"I'm not interested in selling," Jeremy had heard himself say, although until that moment he had not really known just how much he wanted to keep her house.

"Jack Johnson's been renting the pasture land and paying

shares on the crops he grows on the other acreage. I'm sure he'll be glad to continue that arrangement," Randall Bell had said.

Jeremy had nodded. "All right. What about the house? It shouldn't sit empty."

"You're right about that. I heard that your sister's about to get married. If she wants to take Mrs. Warren's best furniture and leave the rest, it'll be easier to rent." Seeing that Jeremy looked a bit overwhelmed at the thought, Mr. Bell had added, "I'll be happy to manage things for you until you finish law school," and Jeremy had quickly agreed to let him take care of the property for a percentage of its income.

Because of that relationship, Randall Bell had stayed in touch with Jeremy and followed his career with interest. A few months ago, when he had found out that Jeremy was considering a return to Rockdale, Mr. Bell had offered him a place in his law firm.

"Jim Barrett's been my partner for years, but since his stroke, he seldom comes to the office, and frankly, I could use some help. Of course, what we handle here can't compare with the kind of bigshot stuff you saw in Birmingham," he had added.

"Good, I hope it doesn't," Jeremy had said earnestly, and their deal was sealed with a handshake.

Jeremy touched his brakes, recalling that the SPEED STRICTLY ENFORCED sign at the outskirts of Rockdale meant just that. He had no intention of marring the first impression he would make with his future constituents by getting a speeding ticket. He coasted across the bridge that spanned Rockdale Creek and came to a stop at the first traffic light. From there, he could barely make out the cupola atop the Rock County Courthouse. Opposite the courthouse on the north side of the square, stood the law office of Bell and Barrett, where Jeremy would start to work on Monday morning.

No one will be there now, he thought, and kept driving straight on Rockdale Boulevard. He stopped for a red light near the post office and was amused to see that two older women, standing on the steps, seemed to be looking him over pretty thoroughly. Jeremy did not recognize them, but he knew they would probably see to it that his arrival was duly and widely noted.

"Everyone knows your business in a small town, but in a way that's good," his mother had once said. "I suspect that fact kept me and a lot of others out of trouble when we were growing up."

Jeremy drove on past a jumble of small businesses, a strip shopping center, and a huge new chain store. He took the next right onto Warren Road, where a billboard proclaimed: MOUNTAIN LOTS FOR SALE, followed by a telephone number.

Jeremy briefly wondered who would buy land on a place as wild as Warren Mountain, then he rounded a sharp curve in the road and slowed to turn into a rutted driveway. Barely legible, the lettering on the battered rural mailbox still read: WARREN.

"The house needs a great deal of work," Randall Bell had warned Jeremy when he learned he planned to move into it. "I'll be glad to get someone out there if you like."

"No, thanks. I intend to do a lot of it myself. I worked several summers for a building contractor," Jeremy had said.

"All right, but you might change your mind when you see it," Randall Bell had said. "I'm afraid the last tenants weren't very good housekeepers."

Jeremy recalled Randall Bell's words when he saw the house where he had known so many happy times. Its once-white clapboards badly needed a coat of paint, the porch swing hung drunkenly on one chain, and a tangle of dead weeds marked the flower garden that had once edged the winter brown bermuda grass lawn.

Nevertheless, something in this old house still said "home" to him as no other place ever could, and Jeremy's breath caught in his throat as he realized that it did, indeed, belong to him. For an instant he fancied that the house seemed to be waiting for him with an air of expectancy, then he shook his head at his foolishness. A house was nothing more than an inanimate object, and this one might cost a great deal more to repair than he had budgeted.

Jeremy got out of the car and slowly walked toward the house. Probably visioning a pillared southern mansion, Guy Pettibone had been enthusiastic when Jeremy told him he would be living in his ancestral home.

"I'll want pictures of you, standing in front of it, holding a paint can and wearing work clothes," he had told Jeremy when he had said that the house needed repairs.

Jeremy knew that it might be some time before the house looked good enough to be in a picture. But, for better or worse, this old place would be his home, at least when he was not in Washington. He would always need to keep a place in his home district, of course.

Jeremy, realizing his presumption, stopped this thought short and ruefully shook his head. *Hubris*, the Greeks called it, an arrogance from excessive pride that had brought down more than one ambitious man.

All right, Jeremy reminded himself, *I won't let myself even think about going to Washington yet.*

He would not, he could not, forget his political goals.

But for now, Jeremy knew that making his house livable and settling into a new way of life in Rockdale would be quite enough to occupy him.

❧

Jeremy's arrival in Rockdale, although unheralded, did not go unnoticed. A strange car always attracted attention, especially if its driver happened to be a lone male. Sally Proffitt and Jenny Suiter, elderly widows and lifelong friends, were standing on the post office steps, exchanging gossip, when they noticed an unfamiliar car, driven by a dark-haired man, stop at a red light. The man was too far-away for them to make out his features, but when the car pulled away and they saw its Birmingham license prefix, Sally and Jenny exchanged knowing glances and nodded.

"That must be the Warren boy," Sally said. "Randall Bell said he'd be coming along any day now."

"I wonder why he left Birmingham? Most young people want to live in cities these days."

Sally shrugged. "Maybe he got in some kind of trouble and had to leave."

"Oh, I doubt that," said Jenny, whose mother and Rebecca Warren had been first cousins, once removed. "Maybe like the Bell girl, he just wanted to come back here to live."

Sally threw her head back and hooted in laughter. "I reckon Joan Bell would like this town even better if she could manage to catch a husband."

Jenny nodded. "She sure hasn't had much luck so far. Maybe her daddy's new law partner will fill the bill."

"I'm sure Randall had that in mind from the start. At any rate, it ought to be interesting to watch what happens."

April Kincaid came out of the post office and stopped for a moment to button her jacket against the chill of the March wind, which was strong enough to ruffle her curly, dark blond hair. Without intending to, April overheard part of the women's conversation and knew they were talking about Mr. Bell, the lawyer, and his daughter, Joan, who had come back to Rockdale to live about the same time that April had arrived. April knew Randall Bell as a lawyer, but although she had seen his daughter around town, they had never met, nor were they likely to.

April dismissed what she had just heard as idle chatter and nodded politely at the women. "Afternoon, Miss Sally, Miss Jenny."

Sally Proffitt returned April's nod. "Hello, April. Does Tom Statum have anything fit to eat tonight?"

It was a question the women asked whenever they saw April, and she always answered them patiently. "Fried chicken's on special, with mashed potatoes and gravy and green beans."

Jenny Suiter made a face. "Ugh! You tell Tom he'd better not try to serve any more of those awful fake mashed potatoes. I could cook up a batch of cardboard that'd taste better."

"And canned green beans would be better than those tasteless frozen things he had last Tuesday night," Sally added.

"I'll be sure to tell Mr. Statum know what you said," April promised.

"You do that, now," said Jenny.

"Yes, ma'am. Goodbye, now."

The women silently watched April thrust her hands into her pockets and walk down the steps.

"Strange girl, that one," Sally said.

"Sure keeps to herself, but she's a good waitress."

"Yes, she is. We'll have to sit at one of her tables tonight."

❧

From the moment her father told her that Jeremy Warren

was coming back to Rockdale, Joan Bell had been looking forward to seeing him again with great anticipation. She vaguely remembered Jeremy as a skinny, dark-haired boy who had spent several summers with his grandmother. When they came into town, Jeremy stayed close to Mrs. Warren, usually too shy or too afraid to play with the Rockdale children. Even when he did, since Jeremy was three years older than Joan and a boy, to boot, their paths rarely crossed.

Joan had been twelve and sick in bed with a cold at the time Jeremy's mother was buried in Rockdale. But even if Joan had been able to go, it was unlikely that her father would have let her. She was away in college when his grandmother had died, and a few months ago, when Jeremy had come to Rockdale to accept her father's invitation to join his practice, Joan was in Huntsville visiting her aunt.

Since she had not seen Jeremy Warren since they had both grown up, Joan had asked her father about him. "How did he turn out? Is he still thin as a rail?"

"Jeremy's slender, but not thin. And now, more than ever, he looks more like the Warrens," he had said.

"Is he handsome?"

Her father had looked amused. "By whose standards? As picky as you are about men, I'm not about to answer that question."

"I'm not 'picky'. . .I just happen to have high standards," Joan had replied.

However, Joan had to admit her father's words held a germ of truth. Even given the fact that most of her friends from college had been in no hurry to get married as soon as they graduated, at the age of twenty-seven, Joan was quite ready to walk down the aisle. That she had not already done so was partly her fault, Joan knew. Several times she thought she had found the right man. She had been engaged twice, once long enough to have to return some early wedding gifts. But each time something had happened to destroy the relationship on which she had pinned her hopes.

"Men today just can't seem to handle commitment," Joan had complained when her last marriage prospect dropped her when she had pressed about his intentions for their future.

"Or maybe they just can't seem to handle you," Randall Bell had replied. "Maybe I shouldn't have tried to be both mother and father to you all these years."

"You know I'd have hated having a stepmother," Joan had said, and her father did not disagree.

Joan had been ten years old when her mother had died, and her father had thrown himself into his work with a zeal that had left little time for anything else. A housekeeper had looked after Joan, and her aunt, who had no children, had been unable or unwilling to let Joan get very close to her. Randall Bell was relieved when Joan went away to college, but last year, when she told him she wanted to return to Rockdale, he had tried to talk her out of it.

"You won't like it. There's nothing in Rockdale for a young woman of your education and talents," he had warned her.

There aren't many eligible men in all of Rock County, Joan knew her father meant, *I know you're disappointed not to be married yet, but coming back here to live isn't likely to make you happy, either.*

Not wanting to think how right her father had been, Joan sighed and picked up a stack of test papers she had put off grading all weekend. She had needed a job, and Mr. Benson, the Rockdale High School principal ever since

Joan could remember, had been delighted to welcome one of their own to his faculty.

"Lucky for us that Mrs. Hobbs decided to retire, after all," he had said. "No telling when I'd ever have another opening in social studies."

Lucky isn't the word for it, Joan thought grimly. Her two classes of seniors had suffered through a semester of economics and now struggled with the mysteries of government, while the overwhelming majority of the sophomores taking world history seemed totally uninterested in the subject.

For the time being, however, the job suited Joan's purpose well enough, at least until the end of the school term. After that, if Rockdale had nothing better to offer, then she would be forced to rethink her situation.

Joan sighed, uncapped her red pen, and had just started to mark the first paper when the telephone rang.

"Don't bother to get up. I'll answer it," Randall Bell told his daughter.

He knows it won't be for me, Joan thought sourly. *Even on a Saturday evening, no one in Rockdale is likely to call to invite me out.*

Her father put his newspaper aside and walked into the kitchen to pick up the phone. Through the open door, Joan could hear the surprise in his voice. "Jeremy! I was wondering when I'd hear from you. Are you still in Birmingham?"

Joan raised her head and listened intently to her father's side of the conversation. From it she concluded that Jeremy Warren had indeed arrived in town and was already making himself at home in his grandmother's house.

"I'm surprised the phone company would activate your service on a Saturday," Joan heard her father say, then,

"Oh, of course. I forgot you have a cellular phone. What are your supper plans?"

Joan put her papers aside and went into the kitchen. She touched her father's arm to get his attention. "You can invite him over here," she said.

Her father glanced at Joan, then frowned into the receiver. "What did you say? Oh, yes, that's a good idea. Try the new grocery on the boulevard. You went past it to get to Warren Road. Yes, that's right. Well, if you can't come tonight, how about meeting at the Club for brunch tomorrow? One o'clock will be fine. I'll see you then."

Randall Bell hung up the telephone and turned to Joan. "That was Jeremy Winter," he said unnecessarily. "He'll be coming to the Club tomorrow for brunch."

Joan made no effort to hide her satisfaction. "I'll look forward to seeing your new partner at long last," she said.

Randall Bell looked at Joan without smiling. "I'm sure you will."

❧

Jeremy followed his sister's advice and put sheets on the sagging mattress in the biggest bedroom as his first order of business, then he took the list of staples she had made and headed for the new supermarket he had passed on the way to the house. He had no trouble finding enough of the kind of food that bachelors favor to stave off starvation, at least for a few days. However, when Jeremy had put the food away, he discovered that the oven in his grandmother's old stove no longer worked, and he realized he would not be able to cook the frozen dinner he had planned to have.

Jeremy sighed. He had not counted on having to buy new appliances, and he felt momentarily depressed. *Did I really do the right thing by coming back here?*

Jeremy looked around the dingy kitchen and marveled

that his grandmother had been able to produce a seemingly endless supply of tasty food using its ancient equipment.

"Our people never give up," his grandmother liked to remind him. "Once a Warren mind is set to do a thing, that thing will be done, even if it takes our last breath."

"I'm not going to give up," Jeremy said aloud. He was just tired and hungry, that was all.

Jeremy considered his options. He had turned down supper at Randall Bell's house, but there were restaurants in Rockdale. He had not seen any fast food outlets, but Jeremy recalled a place downtown that served good, although plain, food.

Jeremy reached for his jacket and tried to recall the restaurant's name. He was heading back toward town on the Rockdale Boulevard when it came to him, and he said it out loud. "Statum's. . .that's what it was. Statum's Family Restaurant."

With the fervent hope that it was still operating, Jeremy turned left at the post office and headed for Center Street.

❧

Night after night, the customers of Statum's Family Restaurant followed the same pattern. What April privately called the senior set always arrived by five o'clock, and sometimes even before, followed soon after by several working couples who could afford to eat out every night. Families with small children tended to come earlier than those with older children, who always wanted their parents to take them to the new pizza place on the boulevard, with its enticing computer games. A few regulars, mostly singles who disliked eating with noisy children, came last of all, even though they took a risk that the day's specials might be out by then.

April Kincaid had worked at Statum's long enough to

know all of the regulars by name. She had quickly learned that Rockdale folks expected such friendliness from her, and even though she had to overcome her natural reserve to do it, April tried to chat with every customer who seemed to want to talk, and that was most of them.

At seven-forty-five on this Saturday evening, the senior set, families with young children, and all but one of the families with older children had come and gone, leaving only a scattered handful of diners. Thinking it unlikely that anyone else would come in, April gathered the condiment holders from the vacant tables and went behind the counter to refill them. She rather liked that part of the job because it meant that she would soon be free to remove her white apron and relax while Mr. Statum and the busboy stacked the chairs on the table and swept and mopped the floor.

April had daily thanked God for leading her to this place and blessing her with this job. Tiring and somewhat dull it might be, when April had needed work, Tom Statum had trusted her enough to let her have it. He was a big, rough man of little education, who had been an army cook. When he retired, he came back to his home town and opened this restaurant. April knew she was not the only one that Tom Statum had helped out over the years, but in return for what he had done for her, she tried to be a conscientious waitress.

April had almost finished her task when Mr. Statum called to her, "You have a customer." She looked up to see a tall, dark-haired man standing just inside the doorway, looking around as if uncertain of what he should do next. He wore jeans and a casual flannel shirt, but his leather jacket and loafers told April that this was no logger.

"Are you still open?" he asked. The way he spoke suggested that he was not from around there. *Perhaps that's why I don't recognize him,* April thought.

April picked up a menu as she came from behind the counter and assumed her automatic welcome-customer smile. "Yes, we are. Booth or table?"

"Booth," he said, and April set the menu on the booth he chose, well away from the other diners.

"I'll be right back to take your order," she said.

Behind the counter once more, April took a long, close look at the man and decided she had definitely never seen him before. His nearly black eyebrows formed a straight line that almost grew together over his dark, expressive eyes. With his square jaw and long, straight nose, this man was not handsome in a traditional sense, but his features had character. *I'd definitely remember meeting someone like him,* she thought.

As she filled a glass with ice and added water and Statum's customary lemon slice garnish, Tom Statum walked over to the newcomer and stuck out his hand in greeting.

"Jeremy Winter! I heard you was comin' back here to live. You gonna be livin' in the old home place?"

"Hello, Mr. Statum. It's good to see you again." Even as he spoke, Jeremy was guessing that this man owned the restaurant. "Yes, although I'm still sort of camping out."

The big man grinned. "Say, if you're gonna live in Rockdale, you have to call me Tom, like everybody else does."

April came to the table with Jeremy's water, and Tom introduced them. "April Kincaid, meet Jeremy Winter. He's gonna be livin' here now."

Although April could have felt a bit uncomfortable shaking the hand he offered, Jeremy Winter's fleeting smile assured her he did not take offense at being introduced to her. "Pleased to meet you," she said.

"Take his order. I can see he can use some fattenin' up."

"We're out of fried chicken, but the meat loaf's good."

Jeremy folded the menu and handed it to April. "Then I'll have meat loaf. . .and whatever goes with it."

April usually asked new customers if they preferred rolls or corn bread, but this time, she decided to bring both and see which he ate first. Then next time, she would know without asking.

"That guy's grandmother was a saint on this earth," Tom told April when she passed Jeremy's order on to the cook. "He was a funny lookin' little kid, but he never gave Miz Warren no trouble."

April was glad when a customer came up to the counter to pay his bill. She did not really want to hear any more praise of Jeremy Winter. Whatever he had been like as a boy, or what he might be like now, should mean absolutely nothing to her.

The Warrens and all their money and all the years they had been one of the most powerful influences in Rockdale all made it more unlikely that any of them, especially anyone like Jeremy Winter, would ever look twice at a nobody like April Kincaid.

Whatever else people might say about me, I know my place, April thought. She felt almost relieved when Mr. Statum told her to go on home, even before the cook had finished assembling Jeremy Warren's order.

"Thanks. It's been a long day," April told him.

She went into the kitchen and untied her apron and tossed it into the laundry bin.

"What kind of bread you want me to put on this meat loaf plate?" asked Sam, the assistant cook.

April hesitated for a moment. Jeremy's speech might not sound distinctly southern, but his roots apparently were.

"Corn bread," she replied, and walked out the back door.

two

Although the Rockdale Country Club had been built on land donated by his great-grandfather and the Warren family had always been members, Jeremy had seldom gone there. His grandmother, who had little patience with what she called "putting on airs," attended the annual Founders' Dinner, but seldom participated in the women's luncheons and parties, which she called time-wasters.

"Women ought to do something useful, not fritter their days away in idleness," Rebecca Warren had said when her daughter suggested that her mother should take more advantage of her membership.

Later, when Jeremy started spending summers in Rockdale, his mother had wanted him to take swimming lessons at the Country Club. "I can teach him myself a whole lot easier," his grandmother had replied, and so she did, in a deep pool made by beavers in a part of Rock Creek that meandered through the Warren land.

My grandmother was quite a woman, Jeremy thought as he guided his car through the twin, native-stone pillars that marked the entrance to the Rockdale Country Club. *They don't make many like her anymore.*

The graveled lot was so full that Jeremy had to park a good distance from the entrance. He did not mind the walk, but he was aware that his dark brown tassel loafers would be covered with fine white dust by the time he reached the sprawling, single-story stone building. He wanted to make the best possible first impression on the people who would see him today, people who would be in a position to help, or hinder, his political ambitions. Accordingly, Jeremy had chosen his clothing with care. Sunday brunch was less formal than an evening dinner, but he suspected that most of the people there would probably have come from church services, so the men would be wearing neckties. Jeremy selected a patterned, brown silk tie, ivory dress shirt, brown wool trousers, and tweed jacket, each approved by Mr. Pettibone's fashion consultant.

His head down against the wind, Jeremy approached the building with the long, loping stride that had helped put him on his high school and college track teams. The thought crossed his mind that he should start working out again. Mr. Pettibone had warned him that campaigning was physically demanding, and although Jeremy knew he was in pretty good shape now, he wanted to stay that way.

I must ask if Rockdale has a gym, he thought, then looked up to see Randall Bell standing in the doorway. He came forward to shake Jeremy's hand and motion him into the stone and cedar foyer.

"Right on time, I see," he noted approvingly. "Come along. Our table is over here."

Many people glanced at them as they entered the dining room, but Mr. Bell did not stop to make any introductions until he reached a table by a glass wall that overlooked the golf course. An attractive young woman with hair almost as dark as Jeremy's own turned and regarded him appraisingly.

"Joan, this is Jeremy Winter. I'm sure you two must have met as children, but you probably don't remember it."

I could never forget meeting anyone so beautiful as you. Jeremy probably would never have spoken the words aloud, even if he and Joan Bell had been alone; it was not his style. He would certainly never say anything like that in the presence of her father, who also happened to be Jeremy's employer.

Be direct, but friendly, Jeremy advised himself as he nodded and extended his hand in greeting.

"Hello, Joan. I'm afraid your father's right. I couldn't have picked you out of a police lineup."

Her low, musical laugh was as easy on his ears as her elegant beauty was on his eyes, and Jeremy liked the way she looked him straight in the eye when, without rising from her seat, she took his hand and shook it briefly.

"What a flattering thing to say!" she said ruefully.

"I can assure you that my daughter has never been in a police lineup in her life." Randall Bell's tone confirmed what Jeremy already suspected: his new employer had many fine qualities, but a sense of humor was not necessarily among them.

Joan looked exasperated. "Oh, Daddy, he knows that," she said. She looked back at Jeremy. "The fact is, I only vaguely remember you as a skinny kid with long black hair."

"Well, at least I got rid of the long hair," Jeremy said.

"Now that you two have been properly introduced, let's proceed to the buffet line. I doubt you'd find a better brunch anywhere than we have right here at the Rockdale Country Club."

When her father pulled back her chair and Joan stood, her height surprised Jeremy. In high heels, she matched his five feet, ten inches; he guessed that in flats, Joan would still be only slightly shorter. As they made their way to the buffet, Jeremy admired the unhurried, natural grace of her walk.

Jeremy usually tried not to form too-quick opinions about people he had just met, especially women, but now he found himself making an exception for Joan Bell. *Not bad,* he thought before another idea presented itself. *She's probably engaged. Or even worse, maybe she's divorced.*

Jeremy did not need Guy Pettibone to tell him that marrying a divorced woman would be a great detriment to any candidate for political office.

"You ought to try the shrimp. As the chef likes to say, they're so fresh they were swimming in the Gulf this time yesterday."

Aware that Joan had spoken to him but not sure what she had said, Jeremy nodded without smiling. Mr. Pettibone had warned him not to smile unless he had a genuine reason. "People don't trust grinners. Some will think you're not serious enough, and others will think you're a phony. When in doubt, always go for wisdom rather than wit."

No one had ever accused Jeremy of being witty, but ever since Mr. Pettibone had cautioned him to be serious, he had felt self-conscious about smiling at all.

"Joan's right," Randall Bell added. "You really ought to try the shrimp."

Belatedly, Jeremy realized what Joan must have said, and knew that not responding to it must have made him appear rude. "I'm sure it's delicious, but I can't eat any kind of shellfish."

"How awful to be allergic to such wonderful food!" Joan exclaimed, and looked at Jeremy as if she meant it.

When they had filled their plates and returned to the table, Jeremy told them the real reason he passed up the shrimp. "Actually, I never had any trouble with shellfish until I picked up a bad case of hepatitis when I was living in the Far East," Jeremy said. "Since then, I can't eat shellfish or drink alcohol. I was told that doing either would make me deathly ill."

Joan's eyes widened in disbelief. "That's terrible! How deprived can one person be?"

Jeremy looked down at his plate, not quite knowing how seriously to take her reaction. He felt relieved when her father spoke, as if for him.

"Jeremy shouldn't feel at all deprived. In fact, this world would be a better place if more people had the same problem."

"I don't know about that, but there'd certainly be a lot more shrimp swimming in the Gulf," Jeremy said. He did not want Joan to think he felt self-righteous about not drinking.

Joan looked at Jeremy in such open admiration that he felt his face warm. "I'm glad there's a sense of humor hiding behind that grim expression, after all," she said.

"I don't mean to look grim," Jeremy began, but Randall Bell interrupted, speaking to his daughter as if Jeremy were not present.

"He can't help it, his mother being a Warren. They all look that way. But when people get to know Jeremy, I'm sure they won't think of him as 'grim.' "

Joan leaned forward to speak to Jeremy, her expression earnest. "Speaking of getting to know people, Daddy and I were talking about that last night. We'd like to have a party here at the Country Club so you can meet some people."

"That would be great," Jeremy said, quite sincerely. He needed an opportunity to rub elbows with the important people in Rockdale, and he knew the Bells' guest list would likely include most, if not all, of them.

Joan smiled. "Then since you have no objections, I'll call the Club manager tomorrow and see what we can work out."

By the time they finished eating, the sky had clouded, and a cold wind blew into the foyer when Jeremy opened the front door.

"Wait here. I'll bring the car around," Randall Bell

instructed Joan when he felt the icy blast.

As her father hurried across the parking lot, Joan turned to Jeremy. "Daddy might not have told you so, but he's really very pleased to have you back in Rockdale."

Jeremy nodded, and Joan smiled slightly and added, "And so am I, Jeremy."

Jeremy intended to murmur something in agreement, but at that moment Randall Bell pulled up to the entrance in his almost-new Cadillac, and Jeremy followed Joan outside to open the car door for her.

"Thanks for the brunch, sir," Jeremy said over the rising wind.

"My pleasure. I'll see you at the office tomorrow morning."

"What time?" Jeremy asked, realizing belatedly that the matter of office hours had never been discussed.

"Eight-thirty," Joan said for her father, who nodded.

The car pulled away, and Jeremy stood staring after it for a moment before he thrust his hands deep into his pockets and, bent against the wind, jogged back to his own car.

&

I think I've made a good start so far, Jeremy told himself that night when he had unpacked the last of the boxes of personal items he had brought from his apartment. He was more certain than ever that he would be able to work with Randall Bell. As for his daughter. . .

Jeremy shook his head in wonder. Joan Bell was an unexpected bonus. Her father had mentioned her to Jeremy in passing, saying his daughter was a teacher and had a master's degree from some out-of-state school, but somehow Jeremy had gotten the impression she did not live in Rockdale. Or perhaps he had told him and Jeremy's mind had just tuned out the information.

At any rate, now that he had met Joan Bell, Jeremy knew

there was no way he could likely tune her out again. In fact, if she proved to meet Guy Pettibone's strict requirements, then Jeremy would no doubt be seeing her a great deal.

Don't count your chickens before they hatch, son. Dreaming's fine, but doing is better.

Here in her house, his grandmother's words seemed to echo from every wall, and Jeremy shook his head at his folly. "Slow and easy wins the race," he said aloud. He intended to achieve his ambitions, all right, but he knew it would not all happen right away.

After all, the incumbent legislator had not yet announced his retirement. But Jeremy wanted to make sure that when the time came, he would be elected to succeed him.

❧

The Rock County courthouse had been built in the 1930s from sand-colored stone cut from the nearby tag end of the Appalachian Mountain chain. Although time and the elements had conspired to dim the building's original elegance, perhaps even to render it unsafe, no Rock County officials had ever managed to find sufficient funds to replace it. In traditional fashion, the square, three-story building had wide entrance doors on each of its four sides. From the basement, where the county's records were stored, to the pigeon-crowded cupola that crowned the building, many things needed to be done, from painting the walls and replacing the ceilings to cleaning and repairing the floors.

When April Kincaid entered the courthouse on the second Friday morning in March, her nose wrinkled at its distinct odor. To April, it smelled somewhat like an old, wooden-floored school building, coupled with the dust given off by the old records, along with something more that she could not quite pin down. All similar institutions, no matter where they were located, seemed to have the same kinds of unique smells, she decided.

I'd know this was a courthouse, even blindfolded and led here at midnight, April thought. She had first learned about the courthouse smell in another place and at another time, a place and time she did not like to think about now.

April ignored the creaky elevator and started up the wide steps, which sagged in the middle. Several boards groaned loudly as they were stepped on, and April idly wondered how many thousands of people had climbed these stairs in the past sixty years. She often counted each step, a holdover from the old days when April did anything she could to keep from thinking about the place where she was and the reason that she was there.

All that had changed, but old habits die hard and, as she arrived, slightly breathless, at the third floor, April could have told anyone who cared that she had just climbed sixty-eight steps, including those leading from the street to the south entrance.

She stopped for a moment, both to recover her breath and to see who already waited outside Judge Wayne Oliver's courtroom.

Mrs. Schmidt isn't here yet, April realized, and felt a tiny spark of hope that she might not come, after all. Neither, however, were Toni and Mrs. Evelyn Trent, the social worker who was responsible for getting her to court on time. Also missing were lawyers representing both sides. April recognized Mr. Benson, the high school principal, and the woman with him, Doris Dodd. As school attendance secretary, her report that Toni was chronically truant was a big part of the girl's present legal troubles.

Knowing that joining them would be awkward, April took a seat on a pewlike bench on the opposite side of the wide hall. A moment later, she heard male voices, then two men entered the hall from stairs opposite those April had used. Even before the older man could introduce the younger to the group that waited outside the courtroom, April recognized them both, and drew in a sharp breath.

She had expected Randall Bell, who had been appointed by the court to represent Toni's interests. When she had talked briefly to him about the case, April had resigned herself to the fact that Mr. Bell would probably merely go through the motions of defending the girl. But April had not expected Mr. Bell's tall, slender new partner to be with him, and she tried to recall his first name from their brief meeting at the restaurant.

He's kin to the Warrens, I remember that. But that wasn't the name Tom called him.

Mr. Bell spoke his name at almost the same moment that April remembered it. "Mrs. Dodd, Mr. Benson, this is Jeremy Winter. He's working with me now, and I've asked Judge Oliver to assign him to the Schmidt case in my place."

April's heart sank. As uninterested as Mr. Bell might have been in representing Toni, at least he knew something about her case. Jeremy Winter might be a great lawyer, but he had been in town only a few days. He certainly had not talked to Toni; the girl would have let April know anything that important.

Jeremy was still shaking Mr. Benson's hand when the courtroom door opened, and Judge Wayne's bailiff motioned them to enter.

They can't do anything without Toni, and she's not here yet, April thought as she followed the others into the smallest courtroom on the third floor.

But Toni was already there, sitting alone at the defendant's table, while Evelyn Trent, the gray-haired investigating social worker, sat at the table on the other side of the room. April noted that the girl had followed her advice and had worn a plain white blouse instead of an old tee shirt with her jeans. With her light brown hair pulled back from her thin face, which was devoid of makeup, Toni appeared even younger than her fifteen years.

The girl did not look up when April joined her, but Toni's tightly clasped hands revealed her tension. *No wonder she's uptight,* April thought, knowing that in only a matter of minutes, the entire course of her future could be decided by strangers.

The bailiff knocked on the judge's chamber door, then called, "All rise," as Judge Wayne Oliver emerged.

The judge's black robe hung loosely on his gaunt frame, and he almost stumbled as he took his place at the bench. *He's too old to be doing this,* April thought as Judge Oliver's penetrating blue eyes swept the courtroom, resting briefly on each of those gathered there. He cleared his throat, then spoke in a strong voice that belied his fragile appearance.

"In the matter of Toni Schmidt, minor, I have here the petition of Mr. Randall Bell, Miss Schmidt's attorney of record, to excuse himself from this case in favor of Mr. Jeremy Winter." The judge looked directly at Jeremy. "Your credentials appear to be in order, Mr. Winter. Mr. Bell's petition is hereby granted."

The judge banged his gavel, and Jeremy immediately rose. "May I address the court, Your Honor?"

"You may, Mr. Winter."

"Sir, as you are aware, I've been in Rockdale for only a short time, and I need more time to study this case. I request a continuance of thirty days."

Thirty days! April glanced at Toni, whose expression did not changed. Toni had learned to mask her emotions, but April knew the girl must be deeply disappointed at this further delay.

"So granted," the judge said so quickly that April knew

he had probably not only anticipated the request, but had already decided to agree to it. "This hearing is set for one month from now, subject to the court calendar."

With a final bang of his gavel, Judge Oliver left the bench. April stood with the others as he retired to his chambers, then turned to Toni, whose careful mask of indifference was beginning to crumble.

"I don't see why they can't go ahead and get this over with," Toni said.

"I know you're disappointed, but having someone new to represent you could be a good thing."

Toni looked past April as the lawyer who had asked for more time to study the case joined them.

"Miss Schmidt, I know you heard me introduce myself to the judge, but in case you didn't catch my name, I'm Jeremy Winter, and I'm pleased to meet you."

He stuck out his hand, and Toni took it without saying anything. From the way Toni looked at him, April knew the girl did not trust this new lawyer. She nodded briefly to acknowledge the introduction, then looked at April as if she expected her to speak for her.

Jeremy's faintly puzzled look told April that he knew they had met, but he did not recall her name. She was about to tell him who she was and where they had met when he suddenly seemed to remember.

"Your name is April, isn't it? I think we met at the Department of Human Resources (DHR)?"

"I'm April Kincaid, but I'm not a social worker."

Jeremy Winter took a small notebook from his coat pocket and repeated her name as he wrote it down. "We have met, though?"

April briefly inclined her head. "Yes, the night you came to Rockdale, as a matter of fact. I wait tables at Statum's."

"Of course!" He made another note, then looked from

April to Toni as if trying to figure out their connection. "Are you two sisters?" he asked, his question coaxing a smile from Toni.

"Not hardly," Toni said. "I got no sisters or brothers, either."

"Toni is my friend." April hoped she did not sound defensive. "We both hoped the hearing would take place today."

"Yes, I understand that. I can see that this case has been pending for a while. But I need time if I'm to do my best for you, Miss Schmidt, and I'm sure your friend would agree that the delay is justified."

Toni shrugged her shoulders and looked faintly bored. "Whatever," she said.

Evelyn Trent, the social worker, who had been engaged in conversation with Doris Dodd, came up beside Toni. "It's time to go now," she said.

"April can take me back," Toni said, but Evelyn Trent shook her head.

"You both know the rules," she said, not unkindly. Then she addressed Jeremy directly. "Here's my card if you need to talk to me about anything. I'm out of the office quite a lot, but if you leave a message, I'll get back to you as soon as I can."

"Thank you, Mrs. Trent. I need to go over a few things with you. I'll want to talk to you, too, Miss Schmidt," he added.

The girl met his level gaze. "My name is Toni," she said.

"Goodbye, Miss Kincaid, Mr. Winter. Come along, Toni," Mrs. Trent said. Without looking again at either Jeremy or April, Toni turned and followed the social worker from the courtroom.

April turned to Jeremy and spoke earnestly. "Toni has a great deal of potential, Mr. Winter. If the State declares her incorrigible and ships her off to reform school, it could ruin her life."

"Please feel free to call me Jeremy," he said. "I'd like to hear your thoughts about the matter. Can we discuss it over a cup of coffee?"

April hesitated, then she glanced at her no-nonsense wristwatch and shook her head. "I don't have time now. I'll be through work after three this afternoon, though."

Jeremy consulted his notebook and shook his head. "Sorry, but I have an appointment that I expect will tie me up all afternoon. Why don't you call the office and make an appointment to see me at your convenience? Here's my card," he added when she looked uncertain.

She nodded slightly. "All right."

"Good. I'll see you soon, then."

April watched him stride away, looking every bit like a young man in a hurry to make it to the top. She glanced at the card, on which raised black letters proclaimed his name:

JEREMY WARREN WINTER, ATTORNEY-AT-LAW
OFFICE HOURS BY APPOINTMENT

Those words were followed by the office's street address and its telephone and fax machine numbers.

"Pretty fancy for Rockdale," April murmured under her breath. She had heard that Jeremy Winter had been a big-shot lawyer in Birmingham, and apparently he had brought his city ways with him. While he handed out engraved business cards, all anyone ever had to do to see Randall Bell was go to his office. Nine times out of ten, he would be there.

April tucked Jeremy's card inside her billfold, which she carried, manlike, in the back pocket of her jeans, and she wondered what had made him come to a nowhere place like Rockdale.

Randall Bell had just ushered a client out of his office when Jeremy returned from the courthouse, and he motioned to him.

"Come in and tell me how the hearing went," he invited.

"It didn't," Jeremy said. "Judge Oliver granted my request for a thirty-day continuance."

"Good. I thought he would. Of course, in this case I don't know that it'll help, but at least you'll have some time to study the facts."

"What are they, exactly?" Jeremy asked. "You told me the State wants to declare the girl incorrigible and send her to the Training School. Why?"

Randall Bell pointed to Jeremy's briefcase. "You can read the file. It seems that the girl's stepmother wants her gone, period, and the State agrees."

"I see. What about April Kincaid?"

The older lawyer looked surprised. "She was there? I didn't see her."

"Yes. I thought they were sisters, but she said she's just Toni's friend. I wondered about the connection."

"As far as I know, they're no kin. In fact, nobody knows much about April Kincaid. She just showed up in town one day and Tom Statum gave her a job. I don't know how she got hooked up with Toni. We talked about the case when I first got it, but she never said why she was so interested in this girl."

"Maybe I'll just ask her," Jeremy said.

"She coming in today?"

"No, but she said she'd make an appointment."

"You'd better tell Edith. She might give her a hard time unless she knows you really want to see her."

"What does your secretary have against April Kincaid? She seems like a nice enough young woman."

"Our secretary," Randall Bell corrected. "Edith doesn't

like pro bono cases. If she thinks a potential client can't pay, she isn't always very accommodating."

Jeremy nodded and made a note to have a talk with their secretary, Edith Westleigh, who had informed him they were distant cousins. "You're some kin to every Westleigh in Rock County," she had said with some asperity. "I wouldn't go bragging about it, though, if I were you. Hardly one in ten of them are worth the gunpowder it'd take to blow them away."

If Edith had not laughed at the sight of his stricken face, Jeremy might have thought that she was serious. But he had soon learned that this crotchety-appearing, long-lost cousin knew every family in the county, and that her judgments about their character seemed to be fairly accurate.

Almost as if she had heard her name mentioned, Edith came to the office door and told Mr. Bell that he had a telephone call. "It's Joan," she added.

Jeremy turned to leave, but Randall Bell motioned for him to stay. "This may concern you," he said, lifting the receiver.

I doubt it, Jeremy thought. Since meeting her the previous Sunday, Jeremy had not seen nor talked to Joan Bell, but her father had told him she had made all the arrangements for a "little party" where Jeremy could be introduced to their friends. "Keep your calendar clear for next Saturday night," Randall Bell had warned.

"I'll do that," Jeremy said, although he did not yet have to worry about dealing with more invitations than he could handle.

Jeremy waited while Randall listened to his daughter for a moment, then said, "Yes, he's standing here right now. Maybe you'd better ask him yourself."

"Ask me what?" Jeremy asked, but Randall Bell handed over the receiver without replying to his question.

"Talk to her. I need to look up a file," Randall said.

"Hello, Joan," Jeremy said.

"I'm glad I caught you," she said, her voice barely audible over the background noise. "I thought you might be ready for some home-cooking by now. Daddy and I would like you to join us for supper tonight."

Jeremy glanced at the picture of Joan Bell on her father's desk and was reminded that she was, indeed, quite attractive. "Are you sure you want to cook tonight? I hear that teachers usually feel pretty done-in by the end of the week."

Her low, melodious laugh sent unexpected chill bumps marching down his back. "That's true, so you won't get anything fancy."

"That suits me," Jeremy said.

A loud buzzing sound startled him, and he had trouble hearing Joan. "Oh, there's the bell. I've got to go to my next class. Come about six-thirty, okay?"

"Fine," Jeremy started to say, just as the telephone line went dead. Apparently, Joan Bell had felt so confident that Jeremy would accept her invitation that she had not even waited to hear him say so.

"My daughter's a strong-willed young woman," Randall Bell had told Jeremy.

I'm strong-willed, too, Jeremy could have said, but did not.

At least in some ways he was strong-willed. He knew what he wanted and had some idea of what he must do to get it. Maybe Joan Bell would play a part in helping Jeremy achieve his ambition. . .or maybe she would not.

Only time will tell, he thought.

But, in the meantime, Jeremy certainly did not intend to turn down an invitation to supper.

three

Jeremy appeared at the Bells' front door promptly at six-thirty, confident that he was appropriately dressed in his chino slacks and long-sleeved sport shirt, topped by a casual sweater. He had thought of bringing flowers, but settled instead for a fresh loaf of french bread from the supermarket bakery.

Joan Bell answered the door herself, trim in black slacks and a plaid sweater under her white chef's apron. She smiled in amusement as she took his offering. "When I said supper would be simple, I didn't mean it wouldn't include bread."

Jeremy matched her light tone. "Well, that's a relief. I presumed you'd furnish the water, but I wasn't so sure about the bread."

"Come in. Daddy's in the den."

"Is that you, Jeremy? Come in," Randall Bell called.

Jeremy sniffed appreciatively. "Something smells good," he said.

"That's my special marinara sauce," Joan said. "All I have to do is drain the pasta and toss the salad, then we'll be ready to eat."

"Can I help you?" Jeremy asked perfunctorily, relieved when she shook her head.

"My daughter doesn't like to have anyone watch her cook," Randall Bell said when Jeremy joined him in the den.

"It's just as well. I'm all thumbs in the kitchen."

"So am I. It was lucky for me that Joan came home just

after I lost my housekeeper. Otherwise, I'd have to be one of Tom Statum's regulars."

"I remember your housekeeper. Wasn't her name Ellie?"

Randall Bell nodded. "That's right. Her sister, Pearl, worked for your grandmother for many years."

"Everyone in Rockdale seems to be related in some way," Jeremy said.

"Yes, but the town's getting more new blood all the time, and that's good."

For some reason, Jeremy thought of April Kincaid. She had not yet made an appointment to see him, but with several weeks to go before Toni Schmidt's hearing, she still had plenty of time to do so.

"At the barbershop this afternoon I heard that some company was looking at sites around Rockdale," Jeremy said.

Randall nodded. "That's right," he said, and began to tell Jeremy what he knew about it.

They were discussing possible ways the county could attract new industry when, a few minutes later, Joan called them into the dining room.

"I thought I was invited to supper," Jeremy observed when he saw that the table was set with what was obviously fine porcelain and sterling silver, with crystal goblets beside each place. "This looks pretty formal to me."

"Maybe so, but there's nothing formal about the food," Joan said.

"Joan enjoys playing hostess with her mother's things," Randall Bell added.

Her father could not see the face Joan made behind his back, but Jeremy did, and he interpreted it to mean, *I'm a grown woman and I'm not playing at anything.* He gave her a sympathetic smile and took the chair Joan indicated, to the right of her father's place at the head of the table.

She sat to her father's left and bowed her head while her father said a perfunctory blessing.

Jeremy had not heard grace said before a meal in years, probably not since his days with his grandmother. *That's a nice touch,* he thought, and was reminded what Mr. Pettibone had said about the necessity for Jeremy to join a church.

"I remember hearing Reverend Jones preach at Grandmother's church," Jeremy said a few minutes later when Joan asked him about people he recalled from his Rockdale summers. "Something about his voice always put me to sleep, but almost as soon as I'd nod off, Grandmother poked me awake with her elbow."

"His sermons must have been pretty dull, all right," Randall Bell said. "Even after he left, the church's membership kept going down. A couple of years ago the remaining members disbanded the congregation and sold the building."

"I'm sorry to hear that," Jeremy said. His grandmother had told him that Warrens had helped to start that church, which she no doubt expected to last for at least another hundred years.

"As the expression goes, if you're looking for a 'church home,' you should come to First," Joan said.

Jeremy did not have to ask her which "First" she meant. There was only one church in Rockdale known by that name, an impressive, old-fashioned red-brick building with a Gothic spire and a large membership.

"You should feel right at home," Randall Bell agreed. "Most of the lawyers go to First."

"So do doctors and bankers and people like that," Joan added.

"Reverend Whitson, the senior minister, keeps his sermons brief and to the point," her father noted.

"That sounds appealing," Jeremy said.

Joan nodded as if something had been settled. "Then come to the eleven o'clock service this Sunday. We sit about halfway down on the right. We'll save a place for you."

"Thanks," Jeremy said. "I was thinking about doing some work around the house, but I'll try to make it."

Randall Bell nodded his approval. "I hope you can. Our clients like to see us in church."

Jeremy looked at Mr. Bell to see if he had intended to make a joke. But Randall Bell was not given to joking, and the man appeared to be perfectly serious. *What a hypocritical thing to say about church attendance,* Jeremy thought, but immediately felt a twinge of guilt as he realized that his own motives were no better.

"Many people have the idea that all lawyers are crooked," Joan said, as if to explain her father's words, and Jeremy knew she must have noticed his reaction.

"Unfortunately, some are," Randall Bell said. He frowned at Joan. "But legal ethics are hardly a suitable topic of conversation for the supper table. I'm sure we can do better."

"As a matter of fact, we can. I'd like to discuss the party with you," Joan said, addressing Jeremy. "Since the invitations need to go to the printer tomorrow, I want to make sure you approve of the arrangements."

"Whatever you plan will be fine. I really appreciate all you're doing for me," Jeremy said.

Joan looked at him without smiling. "It's our pleasure," she said.

Something in her tone told Jeremy that, although she had said "our," Joan would not necessarily be going to all this trouble for her father's new colleague without some other purpose in mind.

Joan Bell has her own agenda, he told himself. Soon, he

supposed, he would find out what it was. In the meantime, unless it was at cross-purposes with his own plans, Jeremy was willing to follow her lead.

∾

On Sunday morning Jeremy slept later than he intended to. He scanned the newspaper headlines while eating a sketchy breakfast of coffee and a stale cinnamon roll, then he got out the new navy blue suit that Guy Pettibone's fashion consultant had directed him to purchase.

"This will be an excellent choice for almost any occasion, from weddings and funerals to cocktail parties and dinner dances. . .anything short of a black tie gala," the consultant had said.

"I presume that would include First Church in Rockdale, Alabama," Jeremy told the full-length mirror on the back of his bedroom door. He had been advised to get a mirror because the fashion consultant had said that seeing himself all at once would alert him to any "grooming problems" he might otherwise miss. "There's no point in buying an expensive suit if you don't know what you look like from head to toe."

Jeremy straightened his tie and regarded the rather serious looking image reflected by his mirror. If it were a photograph, he thought, the caption could read: *Jeremy Winter, sincere and successful.*

Satisfied that his appearance was about as good as it would get, Jeremy picked up his car keys and went out into the pleasant spring morning for the ten-minute drive to First Church.

Almost as soon as Jeremy entered the huge double doorway, he felt a light touch on his arm and turned to see Joan Bell.

No doubt she has a full-length mirror, too, was Jeremy's

first thought. From the top of her head to her well-shod feet, Joan was more than just well-groomed. She was a knockout. Her raspberry red suit had a long jacket and a skirt that ended just below the knee, all of which fit as if it had been tailored for her.

"I was afraid you might not see us," she said.

"I don't think anyone could miss that suit," Jeremy said. He meant his words as a compliment, but she smiled ruefully.

"It is loud, isn't it? But this shade of red is my favorite color, and when I saw it in New York last spring, I couldn't resist it."

"I can see why," Jeremy said with admiration. "So you get your clothes in New York?" he added.

Joan's warm, musical laugh attracted several curious stares, and as if suddenly remembering where they were, she took Jeremy's arm and started toward the sanctuary. "No. Daddy and I went up on one of those whirlwind tours. You know the kind, where you see a couple of plays and visit a few museums."

"And shop," Jeremy added.

"Of course," Joan said, smiling.

They reached Randall Bell's pew with the first notes of an organ prelude. After the men exchanged a quiet greeting, Jeremy settled back between Joan and her father and looked around the church. Rows of cushioned, dark wood pews stretched across the width of the sanctuary. On each side wall were many stained-glass windows, each bearing the name of the family that had paid for them. Even though he was too far away to read any of the captions, Jeremy guessed that both the Bells and Randalls had windows bearing their names. Another stained-glass window, this one round and much more elaborate than the others, was set into the wall behind the altar. Although he had never been in it before, the church's interior seemed comfortably familiar, and Jeremy had no doubt that First Church would fit Mr. Pettibone's idea of "mainstream."

With the last notes of the prelude still reverberating against the lofted ceiling, several vestment-clad men came from a rear doorway and took their places on the dais in front of the altar.

Joan leaned toward Jeremy and started whispering their names to him. "The one in the middle is the senior minister, Vance Whitson," she finished, just as that somewhat rotund man came to the lectern to give a brief invocation. As he returned to his chair, a robed choir filled the loft to one side of the altar and sang another invocation. Then the congregation rose for the first hymn, one that Jeremy had never heard, much less tried to sing.

To his daughter's right, Randall Bell sang with much more enthusiasm than skill, but on Jeremy's left, while her lips seemed to be moving, he could not hear Joan at all. *She probably can't sing very well and doesn't want anyone to know it,* he guessed. In the course of the service, in which it seemed to Jeremy that he must have risen and sat at least two dozen times, Joan joined in on all the spoken responses, but he never heard her sing a note.

The robed choir sang an anthem that featured two soloists, a man and a woman. Both had pleasant voices, but Jeremy had trouble understanding the words both they and the choir were singing. After the special music, the other two ministers on the church staff shared the saying of the prayers and led the responsive readings. However, when the senior minister rose to deliver his sermon, they left the dais to sit in the otherwise empty front row. Jeremy settled back, prepared to listen attentively, but when the minister put on his glasses and began to read the sermon, Jeremy's interest waned. There was nothing particularly wrong with the message (which was, as Randall Bell had indicated, mercifully brief), but even as Jeremy heard the words, he had no idea what they had to do with him, and he felt oddly disappointed.

What did you expect? Jeremy asked himself, a question he could not answer. Maybe he did not really know what else, aside from the value of being seen there, he had hoped to gain from attending First Church, but whatever it was, he had not found it.

When the service ended, Joan and Randall Bell began to introduce Jeremy to some of the other members, a process that continued all the way up the aisle, into the foyer, and even to the parking lot. He met assorted doctors and lawyers, merchants and bankers, most with their families.

"Did I miss anyone?" Jeremy asked when they were finally alone again.

Joan laughed. "A few, but they'll probably be at the Country Club. You are planning to join us for brunch, I hope?"

He hadn't been, but considering the meager fare at his house, Jeremy found the idea appealing. "Yes, but only if you'll let me pay my way this time."

"If you insist," Randall Bell said. "Leave your car here and ride with us."

Once more Jeremy found himself sitting between Randall and Joan Bell. In the much closer confines of the car, Jeremy realized that the aroma he had noticed inside the church had come, not from the altar flowers as he had supposed, but from Joan's perfume.

Pleasant, he thought, and almost asked the name of the scent before he realized that that would undoubtedly be a breach of etiquette.

"Well, what did you think of Reverend Whitson?" Randall Bell asked Jeremy when he had safely maneuvered his Cadillac out of the church's parking lot.

"If brevity is the soul of wit, then I suppose he must be really intelligent," Jeremy said.

Randall Bell's matter-of-fact tone reminded Jeremy once again that the older lawyer seemed almost impervious to any attempt at humor. "Yes, he is, but you heard one of his shorter messages. What did you think about it?"

Jeremy hesitated a moment, then decided he might as well be honest. "I really wasn't sure what he said. Does he always read his sermons?"

"Always," Joan said before her father had a chance to reply. "He says that's the only way he can finish on time. If he preached from notes, we'd no doubt still be there."

"I see," said Jeremy. Deciding it would be diplomatic to change the subject, Jeremy quickly added a comment about one of the people he had spoken to after the service. "It was good to see Mrs. Dinwiddie again. She and my grandmother were always good friends. I thought she'd probably passed on to her reward by now."

"Mrs. Dinwiddie was my first piano teacher," Joan said.

Without smiling, Randall Bell glanced at her. "And last."

Joan sighed. "Oh, Daddy, you didn't have to remind me of that." She turned to Jeremy and added, "I'm afraid I'm hopelessly tone deaf."

"Even so, you could have practiced," her father reminded her. "I'll always believe that you could have mastered the piano if you'd wanted to."

"Well, I didn't."

Randall Bell took his eyes off the road long enough to frown at his daughter. "My mother played the organ at First Church for forty years. We all hoped that Joan would follow in her footsteps."

"You hoped, Daddy. Grandmother Randall knew better when she tried to teach me 'Twinkle, Twinkle, Little Star,' and it came out sounding like 'Yankee Doodle.' "

Both what they said and the tone with which they spoke, told Jeremy that he had managed to spark an old controversy between them, and he suspected that Joan's musical training was not the only thing they did not see the same way. Jeremy had known some male colleagues who had gone back home to live after college, and none had found it easy. Jeremy thought the situation might be different for a daughter, but apparently it was not.

I'd better change the subject again before this gets ugly, Jeremy thought. He had his opportunity almost immediately as the car passed what seemed to be a large estate, barely visible through its massive wrought-iron gates.

"Whose spread is that?" Jeremy asked Randall Bell. *I didn't know anyone in Rockdale had that kind of money,* he added privately.

As if he had understood Jeremy's thoughts, Randall Bell laughed ruefully. "Nobody you'd know. It belongs to a songwriter named Jackie Tyler. He made it big in the music business and for some reason he decided to live here part of the year."

"It's supposed to be quite a showplace, but we've never been inside it," Joan added.

To Jeremy's relief, both father and daughter seemed to be in a better mood when they entered the Country Club. Their progress toward the Bells' usual table slowed as Joan stopped several times to introduce Jeremy to even more people.

"This is my boss, Paul Benson," Joan said when she came to his table.

"We've already met," the high school principal said. He introduced Jeremy to his wife, Sarah, and their teen-aged daughters, Ashley and Audra, who regarded Jeremy with great interest.

"I suppose I'll be seeing you in court," Jeremy said to the principal in parting.

"Don't tell me Mr. Benson's having legal troubles!" Joan said when they reached the table where her father was already seated.

"Of course not. He's a witness in a case I inherited from your father," Jeremy replied. He did not know how much Randall Bell told his daughter about his clients' cases, but he guessed it was very little.

"That's all there is to it," Randall agreed. "And speaking of clients, I just saw Fred Liggett over there. I need to talk to him, and it's impossible to catch him in his office. You two go on to the buffet. Don't wait for me."

However, when Randall Bell left, neither Jeremy nor Joan made a move to rise. Jeremy took advantage of her father's absence to tell Joan something that he would not want Randall Bell to hear.

"I admire Mr. Bell tremendously, and I appreciate all that he's doing for me, but if he were my father, I don't think I could stand to live with him."

Joan's face colored briefly, and she smiled ruefully. "Sometimes, neither can I. Being Daddy's little girl again has its disadvantages."

"For what it's worth, I think you're doing a great job of it," Jeremy said.

"It's worth a lot, coming from you, Jeremy," Joan said. She extended a hand toward him, and for a moment he thought she expected him to shake it, but instead she laid it lightly on his. He turned his palm upward and grasped her hand. He barely had time to press her hand lightly before she quickly withdrew it.

The reason was immediately apparent when Jeremy heard Randall Bell's voice behind him. "I see that you've ignored me, as usual," he said to Joan. "Let's join the line before it gets any longer."

Randall Bell walked away before he could see the almost conspiratorial look that Jeremy and Joan exchanged. However, their glance did not go completely unnoticed.

Ashley Benson's long brown hair screened her face as she leaned over to whisper something in her sister's ear that caused the other girl to look over to the buffet line and giggle.

"It's about time Miss Ding-dong had a boyfriend," Audra whispered back.

Their mother frowned. "Don't whisper in public, girls. It's quite rude."

"What about whispering in private?" Ashley asked. "Is that allowed?"

Mrs. Benson sighed and adopted the expression of a parent who has suffered much and long. "Don't be impudent, Miss Ashley. You and Audra know very well how you ought to behave."

Don't we ever! said the look that Ashley and her year-younger sister exchanged before each murmured a perfunctory, "Yes, ma'am," and resumed eating.

But there was no doubt that tomorrow, everyone at Rockdale High School would hear the news that uppity Miss Bell, who could not catch a man with a rope, was sweet on her daddy's new partner and that the poor sap seemed to feel the same way about her.

four

April Kincaid, her right hand on the telephone, stood behind the counter at Statum's Family Restaurant some two weeks after Jeremy Winter had told her to make an appointment to see him. April had not meant to ignore his request, but she felt a strange reluctance to talk to the intense young lawyer who had inherited Toni's case. At first, since Toni's hearing was still a month away, it was easy to tell herself that there was still plenty of time. In the back of her mind, April thought that Jeremy Winter might return to the restaurant, but he had not.

I'll call his office tomorrow, April promised herself almost daily, but she never did anything about it, until now.

Just as April lifted the receiver to make the call, Mr. Statum came in from the kitchen with a strange look on his face that she could not quite figure out.

"You had a phone call a few minutes ago," he said.

There was nothing unusual about that; April did not have a telephone, and Mr. Statum had never complained about the rare calls she received at his restaurant. He had even urged her to use the restaurant telephone whenever she needed it. But something told April that this call must have been different.

"Who was it from?" she asked.

Tom Statum folded his beefy arms across his chest. "Are you in some kind of trouble, April? I want to know about it if you are."

April's eyes widened in surprised alarm. "What makes

you think that?"

"I hear tell that you and that Schmidt girl are still pretty thick. I know you think you can help her and all of that, but don't let her pull you down again."

Although April felt deeply disappointed at Tom's apparent lack of trust, she put aside her own feelings in her concern for Toni. "Did Toni call? Is that it?"

Tom Statum looked slightly embarrassed. "No. It was Jeremy Winter, the new lawyer fellow. Said he wants to talk to you about the Schmidt girl."

Only when April let out her breath in a long sigh did she realize she must have been holding it. Her relief tempered her annoyance, and she made herself speak deliberately. "I told you that Toni's hearing had been postponed. I also thought you knew Mr. Winter is going to represent her. He just wants to talk to me about it."

Tom Statum had started wiping the counter while April talked, more because he was ashamed to look her in the eye than because the spotless surface needed cleaning, she guessed. April had become quite used to having people avoid looking at her in the past, but she felt hurt that Tom Statum, who by now should know her about as well as she knew herself, could still harbor doubts about April.

She sighed deeply and turned away to begin to clip the Daily Special sheet to the stack of waiting menus. Tom watched April for a moment in silence, then he put down his rag and looked directly at her. "Hey, I'm sorry if I said somethin' I shouldn't. Tell you what. Why don't you go on over to that law office and talk to Jeremy right now? I'll finish the menus."

April was touched by Tom's offer, but she still hesitated. "That's okay. I can go after the lunch rush," she said.

"Go now and you'll be back before it even starts," Tom

said. "You might as well get it over with."

He knows me pretty well, all right, April thought. She tried to tell herself she had no reason to be concerned about talking to Jeremy Winter. He seemed like a nice man, for a lawyer, and she hoped he would try to do more for Toni than Mr. Bell had.

"All right, I will. . .and thanks."

Tom Statum smiled widely. "No problem, April. Now take off that apron and get out of here."

In the kitchen, April hung her apron on its peg, then closed her eyes in silent prayer. *Lord, just help me do and say the right things to help Toni.*

Feeling better, April hurried out to find Jeremy Winter.

❧

Jeremy had made a note to call April Kincaid in two weeks if she had not already come in to see him by then. When Edith Westleigh confirmed that April had not made an appointment, Jeremy decided to call her himself. The file he had inherited from Randall Bell contained only her work number, and when Jeremy called the restaurant, Tom Statum answered and said that April had not come in yet.

After a brief conversation in which Jeremy had asked Tom to tell April that he needed to see her, Jeremy hung up the telephone. At almost the same instant, Randall Bell entered his office and held out a manila file folder.

"If you find yourself with some free time this morning, this needs to be attended to."

Jeremy eyed the folder warily. "Is that the Morgan title thing?" he asked, and was unsurprised when Mr. Bell nodded.

Of all the undesirable chores that Randall Bell had given Jeremy, title searches had been the worst. The oldest records were stored in dusty file boxes on shelves in the courthouse basement. It was impossible to open them without releasing a fine layer of ancient dirt and grit that settled on the searcher's hands, face, and clothing. When Jeremy had completed his first search, he returned to the office as bedraggled and grimy as if he had been mining coal.

"I should have warned you to wear old clothes to do title searches," Mr. Bell had told Jeremy then. "Keep some coveralls or something in the office. Otherwise, you could have a huge dry cleaning bill."

Now Jeremy glanced down at his second-best work outfit, as the consultant had called the dark trousers and lighter sports coat he had chosen to wear that day, and imagined what it would look like after a few hours in the basement archives.

"I can go over as soon as I change. My sweats are in the trunk of my car."

Randall Bell nodded. "Good. It would be a shame to ruin such a nice jacket." He laid the folder on Jeremy's desk and turned to leave, then stopped at the door. "Oh, by the way . . .I'm having lunch at the Club today, so I won't be here when you get back."

"I'll put the folder on your desk, in case I'm tied up this afternoon," Jeremy said.

Randall Bell lifted one eyebrow as if he doubted Jeremy would have much, if anything, to do that afternoon, but he merely nodded and left without further comment.

Jeremy went to the small parking area behind the office and retrieved a gray fleece top and sweat pants from his trunk, then put them on in his office. When he passed her desk on the way out, Edith Westleigh rolled her eyes at Jeremy. "I reckon I know where you're headed," she said.

"To a hearing before the State Supreme Court, of course," Jeremy replied, and was rewarded by a fleeting smile.

A few minutes later, as Jeremy sneezed from the dust raised by the first record book he opened, he tried to tell himself that what he was doing would pay off for him one day. He would not play the part of a small-town lawyer any longer than he had to.

"Slow and easy wins the race," his grandmother had often said to Jeremy when, as a young boy, he became impatient for things he wanted to come to pass at a faster pace. It would take him time to achieve his political ambitions, but Jeremy was convinced that, with Mr. Pettibone's wise counsel, they would be fulfilled.

When I'm elected to Congress, Randall Bell will have to find someone else to do his title searches. Jeremy's satisfaction faded when he saw that the ledger he had wrestled from the shelf was not the one he needed, after all.

Someday, I'll probably look back on all of this and laugh, he told himself as he pushed the book back into its proper place.

Someday. But in the meantime, Jeremy did not find much to laugh about in the present.

❧

Edith Westleigh pulled her glasses down over her nose and peered at April. "Yes?" she asked, her tone suggesting that April might have come there through some great error.

No one can make me feel inferior without my permission, April reminded herself. She drew herself to her full height and lifted her chin. "I'm here to see Mr. Winter," she said with all the authority she could muster.

Edith Westleigh did not look impressed. "Do you have an appointment?"

You know very well I don't. The old April would have said that and more, but the new person she had become understood that putting anyone else down only lowered her own worth. "No, but he left word that he wanted to see me as soon as possible."

I very much doubt that, the secretary's expression said, but her voice remained carefully polite. "I'm sorry, but Mr. Winter isn't in."

April bit her bottom lip, annoyed that she had not thought of that possibility. *I should have had enough sense to call before rushing over here,* she scolded herself, but she made herself speak calmly, nevertheless. "Oh. When will he be back?"

Edith Westleigh picked up a pencil and tapped it against a spiral-bound book lying on the desk. "I'm not sure. Would you like to make an appointment?"

"No." April started to leave, then turned back. "Can you tell me where he went?" April forced herself to smile, and while the secretary did not smile back, she seemed to be thinking about it. "He really needs to see me. He said it was important."

Edith shrugged and nodded toward the courthouse. "Mr. Winter went to search titles in the basement archives. I reckon you can talk to him there, if you don't mind a little dust."

This time April's smile was quite genuine. "Thanks. If I happen to miss Mr. Winter, tell him I came by."

"I'll do that," Edith Westleigh murmured to the young woman's retreating back.

Edith rose from her desk and watched April walk across the street, striding almost like a man.

"She's an odd one, all right," Edith said aloud before she returned to her desk.

❧

April had to ask directions in two different offices before she finally found the room that housed the Rock County

deeds archives. She stood in the doorway for a moment
and waited for her eyes to adjust to the dim light. At first
all she could see were rows and rows of shelves, crowded
with a variety of boxes, files, and ledgers. Then someone
sneezed, and she looked to the right, where a solitary male
figure wearing somewhat rumpled sweat clothes stood
before one of the shelves, apparently trying to balance a
heavy ledger in one hand while he made notes with the
other.

Jeremy Winter, no doubt, April thought, although he certainly did not look much like he did the last time she had
seen him. He sneezed again, his legal pad fell to the floor,
and he sighed heavily as he stooped to retrieve it.

Not wanting to startle him, April approached Jeremy
cautiously and stopped a few feet away. She cleared her
throat and waited for him to notice her. When he took the
ledger to a table wedged against the far wall, April followed him.

"Mr. Winter?"

Even in the dim light, April saw his momentary surprise
when he turned to her. "You're Toni Schmidt's friend," he
said, making almost a question.

"Yes. You said you wanted to talk to me?"

A faint smile twitched the corners of his mouth and
quickly faded. He made a gesture that took in the room
where they stood. "Yes, but in case you haven't noticed,
this isn't my office."

Without smiling, April regarded him. "Mr. Statum
told me I should see you right away, and your secretary
told me where to find you. If you can't talk now—"

"Oh, but I can," Jeremy interrupted. "But I don't have
the Schmidt file with me, and I'm not sure I can remember
everything I wanted to ask you."

April hesitated for a moment, then squared her shoulders. "I have some time to talk now. I'll tell you what I know about Toni, and if there's anything else you need, I reckon I can always come to your office later."

"Fair enough, if you can stand all this dust." Jeremy pulled out a dilapidated office chair from the other side of the desk and motioned for April to sit in it. Then he turned his ancient swivel chair toward her, found a blank page on his legal pad, and uncapped a fountain pen. "For starters, how long have you known Toni Schmidt?"

April looked down at her hands and wiggled her fingers as if counting. "Four or five months, I reckon."

"I understand that you met when she stole some things from your apartment. What was that all about?"

April looked at Jeremy almost beseechingly. "Toni's not a bad girl, Mr. Winter. I knew that the first time I saw her. When she took the things from my apartment, she was desperate."

"That was after she'd run away from home?" Jeremy asked.

April nodded. "It was really cold that night, and she didn't have any way to keep warm. She took an old quilt and a couple of ratty looking blankets and left a note saying she was sorry and she'd return my stuff as soon as she could."

Jeremy scribbled on the pad. "I remember seeing a copy of that note in the file. Didn't the police take her in that same night?"

"Yes. They didn't know she had run away until they found her sleeping in the park down by the creek."

"How long had she been gone from home by then?" Jeremy asked.

"A couple of days. Her stepmother says she didn't report

her missing because Toni told her she was going to stay with a friend. But Toni says that her stepmother knew she'd run away and was glad of it."

"That's not what the official report says."

"Maybe not, but that's what happened. Mrs. Schmidt told the police they should ask Toni where she got the quilt and blankets, since she knew they weren't hers. I had just come home and found my things missing and called the police, so it didn't take them very long to figure out that Toni took them."

"That must be a record for the Rockdale Police Force," Jeremy said dryly. For years Rockdale's citizens had been aware of the department's poor performance. The police kept drunks off the streets and enforced the traffic laws almost too well, but had less success solving Rockdale's infrequent crimes.

Jeremy replaced the cap on his pen and leaned forward slightly, as if he did not want to miss a word of April's response to his next question. He had learned the ploy at the Birmingham law firm and found that it often made his interviewees say much more than they had perhaps intended.

"The bottom line is that Toni Schmidt had a long history of truancy and petty theft even before she broke into your place. Her stepmother claims she can't handle Toni, and she said under oath that she thought Toni would harm herself or others if she stayed in Rockdale. On paper, it seems the State has ample grounds to declare her incorrigible. What can you tell me about Toni that might help us keep that from happening?"

April took a deep breath and leaned forward slightly. In the short time they had been talking about Toni, Jeremy Winter had already shown more interest in her defense than Randall Bell ever did. Somehow, she knew that this young lawyer had the skill to help Toni, if only she could persuade him to use it on her behalf.

"All her life, nobody ever really wanted Toni, and she's always known it. She was six when she watched her mom die of a drug overdose up in Tennessee. No one knew where her daddy was and her mom's relatives wouldn't take her, so Toni was passed around from one foster care place to another."

"Then Mr. Schmidt showed up with a woman he said was his wife," Jeremy said when April paused.

April nodded. "He and Marquita got Toni back, but the woman never liked her. Before long Marquita was getting drunk or high pretty regular. Sometimes, even when she was sober, she'd beat Toni for no reason."

Jeremy frowned, trying to remember the details of the case. "Where was Mr. Schmidt then?"

April shrugged. "Good question. He disappeared for about a year and then showed up one day and he and Marquita had a big fight. She left and he took Toni to his sister's in Chattanooga, where she stayed until her father married this woman named Betty and they all, including three of Betty's children from another marriage, came here to Rockdale."

"How long ago was that?" Jeremy asked.

"Three years, I think. Anyway, Toni and Betty's kids didn't get along with each other from the first. From what she says, the kids would beat up on each other, then tell their mother that Toni hit them. . .stuff like that."

"Hearsay," Jeremy murmured. "Did her father ever try to help Toni during that time?"

"I doubt it, although Toni won't say much about him. He probably didn't know about a lot of things that happened, because he started driving big rigs about a year after they moved here. He'd be gone for weeks at a time. Things finally got so bad that Betty tried to make Toni's aunt take her. Right after that, Toni's father had a wreck in an ice storm up north and died a few weeks later."

Jeremy nodded. "That was about the time Toni started getting into serious trouble. Understandable, considering everything that had happened to her."

April lifted her hands in a gesture of appeal. "Of course. But DHR and the school system just look at what Toni did and hear her stepmother say she's a bad girl and ought to be put away." April's voice shook with her outrage, but her eyes remained dry.

"And of course you don't agree," Jeremy finished for her. "But even if Toni isn't sent to reform school, what sort of life can she have around here with her stepmother?"

April looked surprised. "I thought you'd read the file, Mr. Winter. Whatever it takes, I want to be Toni's guardian."

It was Jeremy's turn to look incredulous, and April found her face warming uncomfortably at his expression. "I guess I missed that part," he said.

"Or maybe Mr. Bell didn't put it in the file to begin with."

"He probably didn't think you were serious. I mean, you're so young yourself."

April raised her chin and looked straight at Jeremy. "I'm ten years older than Toni, and she respects me. Besides, I—" April broke off and looked at her watch, then rose from her chair. "I'm sorry, but I must get back to work."

Jeremy stood and followed her to the door. "Thank you for coming over. I'll call you again after I've reviewed the file," he said.

With anxious eyes, April searched his face. "Do you

think you can keep Toni from going to reform school?"

Jeremy's serious expression did not change. "I can try," he said. "I'll need your help."

April's expression matched his. "You've got it," she said, meaning every word.

ॐ

All the way back to the restaurant, April felt as if she stood poised on the edge of a high cliff. She was just beginning to realize that she would have to answer tough questions about her own past if she applied to be Toni's guardian.

I don't even want to talk to Toni's lawyer about it, April admitted. How could she ever stand up to the facts that would come out in open court?

April closed her eyes briefly. *Lord, I'm out of my depth with this. You're going to have to wade in with me and show me what to do.*

five

The party that Joan Bell and her father held in Jeremy's honor the next Friday evening was, by all accounts, a huge success. Nearly all the invited guests came, the food tasted even better than it looked, and almost everyone seemed convinced that Amos Warren's grandson would be a great asset, not only to Rockdale, but also to Rock County and all of Alabama.

Jeremy knew that Joan Bell was responsible for at least part of his success. He was impressed by the simple elegance of her tailored, emerald green suit and matching, flat-heeled slippers. She had swept her long, dark hair back from her face and held it in place with a flat bow of the same satiny fabric as her suit. Joan stayed close by Jeremy's side all evening, whispering names so that he could impress people by seeming to know them even before they could introduce themselves to him. He had already met quite a few of the guests around town or in the law office or the courthouse. Some he had seen at First Church, and he recalled a few others from his past visits, but at least half were total strangers, with names as unfamiliar as their faces.

"I must have shaken two hundred hands tonight," Jeremy told Joan when the last guest had left the Country Club.

"At least that many people were here," she said.

"How do you remember them all? You'd been away from Rockdale a long time yourself. A lot of new people must have arrived while you were gone."

Joan looked pleased at Jeremy's obvious admiration. "That's true, but then, I've always been a people person. I might have no idea of my checkbook balance, but once I put a name with a face, I'll most likely remember that person forever."

Randall Bell joined them in time to hear Joan's last words and nodded to Jeremy. "When the time comes, you couldn't find a better campaign manager than my daughter. Just have someone else take care of your bank account."

Campaign manager? Jeremy cast Joan a startled look, but she had turned away to frown at her father. *Randall Bell must have told her about my plans,* he thought. They had discussed the possibility that Jeremy might eventually run for some political office, and Randall had agreed that that would be a good idea. Although neither had mentioned any particular race by name, Jeremy suspected that his uncle had already spoken to Randall Bell about Harrison's congressional seat.

"Oh, Daddy, why must you always put me down?"

Heeding the edge of anger in Joan's voice, Randall Bell put a placating hand on her arm. "You're just like your mother. All the Birches are entirely too sensitive. It's no wonder that—" He broke off, apparently thinking better of what he was about to say, and turned his attention to Jeremy. "Sorry. I didn't mean to start a family row. I hope you enjoyed the party."

Jeremy nodded enthusiastically. "Oh, yes, sir. It couldn't have been better. I must have met just about everyone in Rockdale by now."

"You now know most of the people who matter, and that was the idea," Randall Bell said.

"I can't thank you, and Joan, enough," Jeremy said.

Randall glanced at his daughter and nodded. "Yes, Joan must take all the credit for planning the party. My part is paying for it."

As if Mr. Bell's words were his cue, the club manager emerged from his office holding a sheaf of papers. "May I have a word with you, Mr. Bell?" he called.

"I'll be right there." Randall Bell turned to Jeremy. "This could take some time. I don't want to impose on you, Jeremy, but I'd appreciate it if you'd take Joan home. She's had a long day, and I'm sure she's tired."

Jeremy thought of saying that Joan looked almost as fresh as she had when the evening first began, but since Randall Bell's words and tone of voice were very much like those he used when giving him orders at the office, he didn't. "Of course. I'll be happy to see Joan home."

Joan hesitated for a moment as if she wanted to protest, then she thanked Jeremy and shook a warning finger at her father. "Don't stay out too late, now. Remember we have to get up early tomorrow morning."

"As if you'd let me forget," Randall Bell said with some asperity. "I'll see you at the office on Monday, Jeremy."

"Yes, sir."

When Randall Bell walked away from them, Joan took Jeremy's arm and smiled. "Daddy may think I'm on my last legs, but I don't feel a bit tired."

"You don't look it, either. All the same, I'll bring the car to the door," Jeremy said.

Joan's smile was grateful. "All right. I suppose I can handle a little pampering."

On the drive back to the Bells' house, conversation turned to the Bells' weekend plans.

"Daddy has to take a deposition in Memphis, and since my college roommate lives there, I decided to go along."

"It's been a while since I've visited Memphis," Jeremy said. "Does it still have cool blues and hot barbecue?"

Joan laughed. "Jeremy Winter, I do believe you missed

your calling. You sound more like a poet than a lawyer when you talk like that."

Jeremy chuckled. "My old English teachers might disagree."

At the Bells' house, Jeremy got out first and came around to open the door for Joan. It was a small courtesy he had always been willing to offer his female passengers, but few of his dates ever gave him time to do it. Instead, it appeared that they could scarcely wait until the car stopped before getting out, often even before Jeremy had unbuckled his seat belt.

"I wish you were going to Memphis with us," Joan said when they reached her front door and she handed Jeremy the key. He unlocked and opened the door for her, but made no move to step inside until she turned back and tugged on his sleeve.

He followed her into the dimly lit foyer and tried to picture himself in Memphis with Joan Bell and her father. *I already see quite enough of Randall Bell in the office,* Jeremy decided.

"I have so much to do around the house, I can't even think about going anywhere yet," he said.

"In that case, you'll just have to settle for a taste of that good barbecue. I'll bring you a sack of ribs."

"That sounds good," Jeremy said. "Have a safe trip . . .and thanks again for the party."

Jeremy's hand already grasped the doorknob, and he had every intention of turning it, opening the door, and leaving. But before he could do so, Joan put her hands on his shoulders and moved toward him. She was kissing his lips almost before Jeremy realized that she intended to do so. The subtle scent of her perfume seemed to reach out to envelop him. Reflexively, without thinking, Jeremy put his left arm around Joan's waist and pulled her even closer, cradling the back of her neck as he returned the kiss.

Joan, who had initiated it, ended the kiss a breathless moment later. She stepped out of Jeremy's embrace and opened the front door. "Good night, Jeremy," she said matter-of-factly. "I'll see you next week."

"I suppose so," he murmured. As the door closed behind him, Jeremy thought he heard Joan's warm laugh, and he wondered what she really thought about him.

Something's not exactly as it ought to be, he told himself, but Jeremy suddenly felt too tired to worry about it. Her father had said Joan would make a good campaign manager, but Jeremy thought Randall Bell might have had another, more important role in mind for her all along.

This is my daughter, Joan. Congressman Winter's wife, you know.

Jeremy shook his head at the image his mind had conjured, climbed back into his car, and pulled away from the Bells' house without a backward look.

Even if Jeremy had looked back, he could not have seen Joan at a window in the dark living room, watching to see what he would do.

"When a man looks back, it's a good sign he'll soon return," Joan had always heard.

Joan turned away from the window and touched her fingertips to her lips, which still tingled from the warmth of Jeremy's kiss.

Jeremy Winter isn't going anywhere. I'll see him again. And the next time he leaves this house, I'll make sure he looks back.

❧

On Saturday morning, Jeremy's clock radio came on at the usual time, but instead of music, Jeremy awakened to what seemed to be a local call-in talk show. Before he could stretch far enough to turn it off, he realized that the topic of conversation seemed to be Congressman Harrison, the man who currently represented the Rockdale part of Alabama in Congress.

"I jest wanted ter say that I used ter think that Mr. Harrison was doin' a good job fer us, but of late it seems like he'd ruther stay up there in Washington City than come home an' see what we need down here. I mean, what's he there fer, anyhow?" a man drawled.

Jeremy heard a faint click as the radio announcer disconnected that caller and spoke to the radio audience. "Well, folks, you just heard that feller say that Representative Harrison ought to be replaced. What about it? Anybody out there want to say anything else about our representative?"

After a slight silence, an obviously toothless elderly woman came on the line. "Is this the Call and Tell line?"

"Yes, ma'am, you're on the air. Go ahead with your comment."

"I think Mr. Harrison is a fine man and I hear the reason he don't come back much no more is 'cause he's been real sick. Look at him next time he does one of them talks of his'n on the TV an' you'll see. The man looks bad."

Jeremy recalled that his grandmother had sometimes said that someone "looked bad." "Mark my words, they might as well go on and call the undertaker," she would say, and usually she was right.

"Thank you, ma'am. I'm afraid we're out of time for this week's Call and Tell show. Thanks to all of you who called in, and to those of you who didn't get on the air this time, remember we'll be back again next Saturday morning, live from WRCK, located right here in Rockdale, Alabama, the heart of Rock County. Thanks to our fine sponsors. . ."

Now wide awake, Jeremy sat up and turned off the radio. As he dressed in work jeans and an old tee shirt, he considered the implications of what he had just heard. The rumor that Representative Harrison might be ill had surfaced in Washington several months ago, but apparently the people in his own district were the last to know.

If he's really that sick, he might have to resign before the next election, Jeremy thought. That did not necessarily bode well for him, since Mr. Pettibone had pointed out that Jeremy would need time to build a base of support for his candidacy.

I'll call him Monday and see what he thinks I should do, Jeremy decided.

After making a sketchy breakfast, Jeremy retrieved some gardening tools from the shed behind the house and took them to what had once been a flower bed.

Poor Grandmother, Jeremy thought when he saw how weeds had all but choked out the old roses she had loved so well.

"Thorny they are, Jeremy, but beautiful enough to make up for it." she would say when he complained about the scratches he got helping her prune them.

"It seems to me they'd be even prettier if they didn't have so many stickers," he would say.

"Nothing beautiful comes without some price," she had told him.

As he did with most of his grandmother's sayings, Jeremy had dismissed her words as having nothing to do with his life. *When I grow up, I won't plant anything like these dumb old roses. If I can't have roses without thorns, then I won't have them at all.*

Recalling the obstinate boy he had once been, Jeremy shook his head. He pulled on thick work gloves and bent to examine the plants. When he pulled away a tangle of dead grass and last fall's leaves, he saw that, despite their many dead canes, the plants had already begun to put out tender green shoots.

"I think we can save them, Grandmother," he said aloud. It was something that Jeremy had found himself doing ever since he had come back to Rockdale. He knew she was not actually there, of course, and wherever she was, she probably could not hear him, anyway. But a sense of her love for Jeremy was almost palpable everywhere he looked, and he did not feel the slightest bit odd or self-conscious when, at times, he felt compelled to share a thought or two with his grandmother.

Even though his muscles painfully protested that they were unused to such hard labor, Jeremy worked steadily all morning. At noon, he went inside for a sandwich, which he ate standing at the sink. He looked out the window and noticed how Warren Mountain, which rose to a height of some 900 feet, had already begun to show signs that the cold, hard winter was about to yield to warmer weather. A hazy golden green tipped the hardwood trees and shrubs near the base of the mountain. Although he had seldom come here in the spring, Jeremy knew that the "bloom line" would, day by day, make its slow advance upward, until the entire hill took on the same golden green hue, followed by a similar progression of darker shades of green as the trees became fully leafed out by early May.

This really is a beautiful place, Jeremy thought. He had lived and traveled literally all over the world, but he had never seen anything that could match the natural beauty of the mountains, lakes, and valleys right here in Rock County, Alabama. "This area has to be the best kept secret in the whole United States," his mother would say every time she came back to visit. "Why would anyone want to live anywhere else?"

Why, indeed, Jeremy thought. Suddenly reminded of his mother, Jeremy finished his sandwich and decided he had done enough yard work for one day. He showered, put on fresh jeans, combed down his hair, which looked even blacker when it was wet, and walked down the main road to a narrow graveled road that led to the Warren family cemetery.

The small graveyard nestled on a flat plateau between two hills on the east side of Warren Mountain about a half mile from the house. Someone—Jeremy thought it was probably his great-great-great-grandfather—had left enough money to erect a stone fence around it and had established a fund for the cemetery's continued maintenance.

With relief Jeremy noted that the graves had obviously been recently tended and looked neat. Randall Bell had been seeing to the cemetery since Rebecca Warren's death, and apparently he had done a good job.

That's something I ought to be doing myself now, he thought, and made a mental note to speak to Mr. Bell about it. Buried here were Warrens and Ridings and Westleighs and Winters; there was not a single Bell or Randall among them. The Warrens were Jeremy's family, and it was his responsibility to tend their final resting place.

Although his family had never felt a need to visit the cemetery as a means of staying in touch with their loved ones, they always went on Decoration Day, the last Sunday in May. In a kind of minifamily reunion, as many as could get there arrived at the cemetery with fresh or dried flowers—they would have nothing to do with anything artificial—for each grave. The oldest surviving family member present would tell the younger children about their ancestors buried there. Then they all went to church, and after the service, the women would set out on plank-and-sawhorse tables the covered dishes that each family had brought. Everyone spent hours eating and "visiting," then back at the house, Rebecca Warren would offer everyone sandwiches, pound cake, and iced tea, and although they all said they were too full to eat another bite, the food had somehow disappeared.

Jeremy smiled at the memory, which seemed to have happened a very long time ago. He had attended several such Decoration Days when his father was stationed only a few hours' drive away in Georgia. His grandmother had always been a sort of grand marshal for the event, and the family's participation in the tradition had ended with her death.

We should do it again this year, Jeremy thought, even before he recalled that Mr. Pettibone had advised him to have a family reunion. Then Jeremy shook his head as he realized the impossibility of arranging anything like that on such short notice, and with the house still needing so much work to make it presentable.

But by next year I ought to be able to swing it, Jeremy thought.

He began a slow circuit of the cemetery, pausing before each grave as he tried to remember how he was related to the people whose names he could barely read on the weathered headstones. The oldest stones were almost illegible, and Jeremy made another note to ask Randall Bell if anyone had information about the people who were buried there.

At his grandmother's grave, Jeremy stopped and read the inscription on her headstone aloud: "A woman of wise counsel who feared the Lord."

Quite a tribute, he thought, *and absolutely true*. Rebecca Warren never took on anything without asking for God's approval.

When Jeremy sighed and stepped away from the tall marker, he heard a muffled cry. He looked up, surprised to see that a young, blond woman stood a few feet away, equally astonished.

"Mr. Winter!" she exclaimed at the same time that Jeremy tentatively spoke her name.

"April Kincaid?"

Her face reddened and she spread her hands wide as if to apologize for the intrusion. "I'm so sorry. I didn't know anyone was here. I reckon I'm trespassing."

She looked so anxious that Jeremy hastened to reassure her that she had done nothing wrong. "The sign says, 'Posted—No Hunting,' so you're all right."

When she still looked as if she doubted it, he added, "Of course, if it did say 'No Trespassing,' I'd have to shoot you."

She smiled then, a small upturning of her mouth that faded all too soon, and Jeremy realized that he had never really noticed what a nice smile she had.

"I'm sure it would be justifiable homicide. Isn't that what you lawyers call it?" April asked.

Jeremy nodded and tried not to stare at her. *There's something different about her today,* he thought, but could not decide exactly what. Instead of being pulled back from her face, April's hair hung in tight curls around her face, half-screening it when she ducked her head in embarrassment. And instead of the uniform she wore to wait tables at Statum's, April had on a well-fitting pair of blue jeans, topped by a turtleneck jersey in a light shade of brown that made Jeremy realize that April's eyes were the same warm color as hazelnuts.

"How did you get here?" Jeremy asked, breaking off his gaze to look past her at the graveled lane. "I didn't hear a car."

April almost laughed, but managed to stifle the sound at the last minute, as if she did not want to appear to be rude. "That's because I don't have one," she said. "I rode my mountain bike," she added when Jeremy seemed puzzled that she would walk so far.

"I take it you've come here before," he said, making it a question.

She nodded. "I came upon it by accident the first time I

rode my bike all the way to the top of Warren Mountain. It's such a beautiful place, and there's something so. . . calming about it that I've been back several times since. I didn't know it belonged to you. I hope you don't mind."

"It doesn't belong to me, exactly," Jeremy said quickly at the anxious tone that had crept back into her voice.

"But these are all your people, aren't they?" April's broad gesture took in the nearby graves.

"Yes. My grandmother and grandfather are buried side by side over there, and the newest headstone marks my mother's grave."

"Oh," April said, and once more looked distressed. "I'm sorry. . .I had no idea. . .I'll go now," she said, and turned to match action to her words.

"You don't have to leave," Jeremy said. "You can stay here as long as you like and come back whenever you want to. It's fine. . .really."

April bobbed her head to acknowledge his invitation. "Thanks. I don't have much time, that's for sure. I usually spend Saturday with Toni, but she had to baby sit today."

Jeremy looked surprised. "Baby sit? Does she do that to earn money?"

The guarded look returned to April's face, and she shook her head. "Not hardly. DHR put her in foster care with the Potters. They have two of their own and two other fosters besides Toni. Since she's the oldest, she has to take care of the others when the Potters go somewhere."

Jeremy frowned. "Is that legal?" he asked.

April's sudden laugh startled him. "Mr. Winter, you're the lawyer, remember? I reckon you ought to know that if anybody would."

"I don't know much about family law," Jeremy admitted.

"What kind of law did you study?" she asked.

"I worked with business contracts in Birmingham, but since I got here, I've done a little bit of everything."

"Like title searches," April said.

"Yes. And that reminds me we should talk some more about Toni's hearing." Jeremy motioned toward a section of the graveyard fence that was flat enough to sit on. "We can sit over there and discuss it now if you have the time."

April hesitated, then she glanced at her watch and shook her head. "I'm sorry, Mr. Winter, but I have to work tonight. I'd better start on back to town."

"I'm sorry you can't stay." Jeremy was somewhat surprised to find that he meant it. "I need to interview Toni next week. I'd like for you to be there, if possible."

April nodded. "I'd like that, too."

"I'll look at my schedule and see when we can set it up. I'll let you know when it'll be."

"Thanks, Mr. Winter. I reckon I'll be seeing you, then."

When April turned and started to walk away, Jeremy caught up with her and stopped her. "Wait. There's one more thing."

She looked at him, her hazel eyes betraying her apprehension. "What's that?"

"My name. . . It's Jeremy. I'm not old enough to be 'Mr. Winter.' "

April's small smile returned, then vanished. "All right." She got on her bike and put on her helmet, then looked back at the cemetery. "You don't know how lucky you are to have a family like this," she said in a low voice, then rode away.

"What did you say?" Jeremy called after her, but if April heard him, she gave no sign.

Jeremy stood and looked down the graveled lane a long time after April's black mountain bike had disappeared from view.

I won't mind seeing her again, Jeremy realized.

six

With little enthusiasm, Jeremy climbed out of bed the next morning, a cloudy Sunday, and dressed to go to First Church. But when he came to the intersection that would take him to town if he turned left, he turned right instead and drove toward the church where his grandmother and her family before her had worshipped every Sunday.

He knew the building would not look the same, even if it still stood; Randall Bell had said the congregation had disbanded. *It's probably deserted and boarded up,* Jeremy told himself. However, members of his family had started the church, and even though it no longer existed, he felt a compulsion to see it for himself.

"This doesn't look like the same place," Jeremy said aloud a few minutes later when he came to a much larger parking lot than he remembered and saw groups of people, both families and individuals, heading for a rambling structure whose original white frame building had obviously been enlarged with additions on both sides to the rear. The weather-beaten wooden signboard was gone, replaced by one of sturdy metal and fiberglass, with space for changeable messages. Jeremy slowed his car and read it:

ROCKDALE COMMUNITY CHURCH
PROCLAIMING CHRIST IN HOLY BOLDNESS
ALL ARE WELCOME
ED HURLEY, PASTOR

His curiosity aroused, Jeremy turned into the graveled

parking lot, over which a layer of fine white dust hung like morning fog, and parked at the end of the row closest to the building. He had no more than gotten out of the car when someone he did not recognize spoke to him, and nearly everyone else he encountered on his way to the church also greeted him. The men shook Jeremy's hand and smiled as if they were really glad to see him, although it was obvious that none of them knew him or realized his connection to their church. The greetings continued into the building itself, where Jeremy saw Tom Statum, the first person whose name he could call.

"Hello, Jeremy," Tom said as they shook hands. "I thought you might come and see what we've made of this place."

"I didn't really know anything about it," Jeremy confessed. "I heard that Grandmother's old church had disbanded, but all of this is a surprise."

"Nobody invited you? Now, that's a real shame," Tom said. He looked as if he had more to say on the subject, but just then a piano began a quiet prelude, and everyone, including the many small children already seated inside the auditorium, immediately quieted.

Tom remained at the door, Jeremy supposed to greet late arrivals, and Jeremy took a moment to survey the old church's interior. Just as he remembered it, the plain clapboards were painted white, and the side windows still had their original panes of brightly colored Italian flash glass, which let in more light than traditional stained-glass windows. The elaborate old carved pulpit and upholstered chairs behind it were gone, replaced by a modern-looking lectern, but the same graceful cherry wood rail still curved around the altar.

As if it had only been a few weeks instead of many years, Jeremy clearly recalled the smoothness of the wood against his hands and forehead as he had knelt there beside his mother and grandmother. Jeremy had really prayed then, something that he had done less and less in the years since.

Almost automatically Jeremy sought out the pew where his grandmother always sat, the fourth from the front on the right of the center aisle. Jeremy edged past a family with several young children to take his old place near the end. As if to welcome him back, the morning sun suddenly broke through the clouds and sent its beams streaming into the church. Just as he had done as a boy, Jeremy held his hand out to let the rays fall across it, so that his skin appeared in turn to be blue, then yellow, then red.

Jeremy heard a giggle and looked to his left where a little girl who appeared to be about six or seven gleefully imitated his action.

"I can make colors too," she told Jeremy before her mother shushed her.

Jeremy smiled at her, then returned his attention to the front of the church, where two men now sat on rather plain chairs behind the pulpit. The older, who had startling white hair and dark eyes, Jeremy assumed to be the pastor, Ed Hurley, according to the sign out front. The younger man, his thin frame topped by wiry red hair, came to the pulpit first and signaled for the congregation to stand. He nodded to the female pianist, who launched into a lively chorus that everyone seemed to know, something about this being the day that the Lord had made.

These people sing as if they really mean the words, Jeremy thought. Then, with almost no break, the tune changed and everyone began a second, quite different, chorus.

"There, mister." The little girl beside Jeremy tugged on his sleeve and pointed to a folder marked "Choruses" in the pew rack in front of him, but by the time he finally found the one they were singing, the music changed yet again. Although Jeremy had never heard it before, he found the slow, haunting, sweet melody deeply affecting.

"We are standing on holy ground. . .and I know that there
are angels all around. . . . Let us praise Jesus now
. . . . We are standing on holy ground. . . ." *

As they repeated the chorus, Jeremy noticed that many
of the worshipers had closed their eyes and held up one or
both of their hands. Jeremy tried to imagine the people in
First Church becoming so involved in their worship and
could not.

After the choruses, the pastor came to the pulpit and
motioned for everyone to be seated. "Let us pray," he said.

Just before he bowed his head, Jeremy was surprised to
see that the pastor and many of the congregation actually
knelt. The prayer itself was also different from what Jeremy
expected. Rather than the usual self-conscious exhortations,
this pastor almost seemed to be in earnest conversation with
a God he obviously revered too much to shout at.

The red-headed song director rose to lead another hymn,
which Jeremy knew well enough to sing without looking at
the hymnal. On the final chorus, Tom Statum and the other
ushers came down the aisle bearing the offering plates.
After one of the men offered a brief prayer that the money
would be used in God's Will and to His glory, they began
to collect the offering.

Occupied with taking out his wallet and removing some
bills, Jeremy did not look back at the pulpit for some time.
But, when the first soaring notes of a taped accompaniment
got his attention, Jeremy looked up at the singer.

With an almost physical jolt, Jeremy realized two things
at once: that the singer had a beautiful voice—and that she
was April Kincaid.

Jeremy could not stop staring at her. April wore a simple
beige dress with long, full sleeves that fell back from her

arms as she raised her hands, palms out, in a gesture similar to the one that Jeremy had seen so many others use that morning. She sang with her head thrown slightly back and her eyes half-closed. Even without being amplified by a microphone, April's surprisingly rich and clear soprano filled the auditorium with glorious sound.

Unlike the soloists at First, April made each word clear, singing with such obvious conviction that Jeremy knew the sentiments must come from her heart.

When she sang about God's grace, every person in the room felt its power and presence among them. As April sang of being redeemed from her sins, some wept openly. She held them all, including Jeremy, spellbound, and when her solo concluded on a steadily sustained high note of triumph, there was a moment of stunned silence. Then, as if they had all been holding their breath for her, everyone exhaled, and from all around the room came cries of, "Praise the Lord!" and, "Amen!" and, "Hallelujah!"

April left the dais with her head down, as if reluctant to acknowledge their praise. Pastor Hurley waited until she had taken a seat in the front row before he stood and came to the pulpit.

"Thank you, April. That was a greater sermon than anything I'll say today. However," he added dryly, "I did prepare a few concluding remarks."

A ripple of laughter ran through the congregation, which then settled back in anticipation.

From where he sat, Jeremy could see only part of the back of April's head, and he had no idea if she had seen him. *Maybe she doesn't know I'm here yet but she will,* he thought. Each time he had seen April Kincaid, she had seemed different, but hearing her sing today had been Jeremy's biggest surprise so far.

There's something that April isn't telling me about herself, he thought, trying not to keep staring at the pew where she sat.

When Pastor Hurley began to speak, Jeremy gave his full attention to what turned out to be a refreshingly different sermon. Although he regularly cited verses from the open Bible he held in one hand, Pastor Hurley did not consult any notes, but spoke with a spontaneous enthusiasm and sincerity that made everything he said seem even more appealing.

On this Palm Sunday, the pastor read from several Gospels the story of Christ's triumphal entry into Jerusalem, then he invited his listeners to picture themselves as part of the crowd that greeted Christ in Jerusalem.

"Maybe you're there out of curiosity to see this Man Who had done so many startling things. Or maybe it's because you sense that Someone Who just raised Lazarus from the dead and Who had made the blind see and the dumb speak and the deaf hear could also make your life better. If you heard that Someone with power like that was coming into Rockdale today, wouldn't you want to get in on it? Hey, I'd be first in line!"

He went on to say that the same Power that Christ had shown in his days on earth was still available to all who believed that Jesus was, indeed, the Son of God, and that He still lived in the hearts and souls of those who accepted His salvation.

The message put a new and practical slant on a story that had long been familiar to Jeremy, ending in a prayer that included a plea for anyone who had never known what it was to trust in the Lord to accept His invitation to do so.

A young married couple and a teen-aged girl came forward and, after greeting them, the pastor announced there would be two special Easter services the following Sunday. He prayed again, and after a last resounding "Amen" from the congregation, the service concluded.

Jeremy wanted to find and speak to April, but he lost sight of her when so many people stopped to introduce themselves and talk to him. When he was finally free to look for her, April had disappeared. He went outside, searching the dwindling cars in the parking lot, but to no effect—April was nowhere to be seen.

"You got car trouble?" Tom Statum asked when he came outside and saw Jeremy standing alone in the parking lot.

Jeremy briefly debated if he should admit that he was looking for April, then decided against it. "No, I'm on my way to the car now."

They were joined by a short, somewhat plump woman with merry, bright eyes whom Tom introduced as his wife, Jeanette.

Mrs. Statum nodded and smiled. "I've heard a lot about you, young man."

"Good, I hope," Jeremy said.

"So far. But in a town like Rockdale, everybody knows your business. Even think about doing something, and it's all over town before you can say 'Jack Robinson.' "

"I'll remember that," Jeremy said. "Nice to meet you, Mrs. Statum. Good-bye, Tom."

Tom stuck out his hand to be shaken. "Good-bye, Jeremy. I hope you'll come back next week. Being Easter, we'll have a real special service."

It will be special if April Kincaid sings again. The thought came to Jeremy's mind immediately, but his better judgment told him that if he said so, the whole town would hear that Jeremy Winter was smitten with Tom Statum's strange little waitress.

Instead, Jeremy responded to Tom's invitation with a noncommittal nod, then turned and started back to his car. Even as he put the key into the ignition, Jeremy scanned the parking lot once more, still hoping to see April. Then he remembered that she had said she did not have a car, and it was highly unlikely that she would ride her bicycle in her Sunday clothes. Therefore, April had no doubt already been given a ride home.

Jeremy was waiting for the traffic to clear so he could leave the parking lot when he idly glanced in the rear-view mirror and saw the red-headed song leader come out of the church with April beside him.

The sight evoked a strange sensation that Jeremy scarcely understood. Was the man taking April home as a professional courtesy? Or did he have a more personal interest in her? Jeremy tried to recall if the song leader had worn a wedding band, and could not.

It's none of my concern, Jeremy told himself, but his actions betrayed him when he brought his foot down hard on the accelerator, and his tires scratched gravel as the car roared out into the road.

"Who was that?" Ted Brown frowned through the windshield of his ten-year-old Chevrolet at the car speeding away from the church parking lot.

April had caught only a glimpse of the figure behind the wheel, but enough to recognize him. *I'd know Jeremy Winter anywhere,* she admitted to herself, but would never say to anyone else. The thought that he had probably been in church and had heard her sing made April feel oddly uneasy.

"Someone in a big hurry," April said. That much was true, and nothing would be gained by telling Ted Brown that the man was Jeremy Winter.

"That's one of the things wrong with the world today," Ted said. "Everyone's always in such a big hurry to get somewhere else they don't enjoy being where they are right now."

Where does Jeremy Winter want to go? April wondered, then sighed. Wherever it was, he certainly would not be taking her along.

ॐ

Early Monday morning, Jeremy arrived at the office hoping to talk to Guy Pettibone before Randall Bell came in.

"He's out of the office until ten o'clock," Mr. Pettibone's secretary told Jeremy. "Shall I have him call you back?"

"Yes, do that," Jeremy said. Ten o'clock in Washington would be nine o'clock in Rockdale; perhaps he and Mr. Pettibone could still transact their business before Mr. Bell stuck his head into Jeremy's office to discuss that day's work.

While he waited for the call, Jeremy opened Toni Schmidt's file and started making a few preliminary notes about her case. When the time came for him to stand before the judge and argue that Toni should not be sent to reform school, he wanted to be prepared. Seeing April's name in the file, Jeremy was again reminded of her growing appeal to him.

Am I more interested in this case for Toni's sake or for April's?

Jeremy sighed and shook his head in an attempt to stop himself from thinking about April. In order to attain the goals that would ultimately take him far from Rockdale, Jeremy first had to gain the trust of the local people. As Jeanette Statum had said the day before, his every move would be the subject of endless speculation, and even more so after his political ambitions came to light. Jeremy did not have to be told that being linked with a woman like April Kincaid could very well undo the work that he had already done, with the help of Joan and Randall Bell, to put himself in a favorable light with the people who mattered.

But all of that is still in the future, he told himself. *I can't be concerned with more than one thing at a time.*

Jeremy returned his attention to Toni Schmidt's file and

he had taken almost two pages of notes before Guy Pettibone returned his call.

"I heard something that I thought you should know," Jeremy said without preamble.

"I know," Mr. Pettibone said. "It looks like Harrison might resign. If so, someone will be appointed to fill out the rest of his term. That could mean trouble."

"I realize that but what can we do about it?"

After a short silence, Guy Pettibone spoke again. "I'll make a few calls and get back to you. How are things going down there? Any action on the list?"

Jeremy did not have to ask his political consultant what "list" he meant. "I've gotten in touch with some relatives, and I've found a likely church."

"What about the other? Any progress with the wife thing?"

The wife thing? Jeremy stifled his impulse to laugh; the whole idea really was quite preposterous. "I'm sort of see-ing someone," Jeremy said.

Mr. Pettibone made a growling sound. "Sort of? There shouldn't be any 'sort of' about it. You need a suitable wife, and soon. Get on with it."

"Yes, sir," Jeremy said. "Is there anything else I should do now?"

"Just sit tight. I'll make a few inquiries and get back to you."

Jeremy hung up the telephone, which rang again almost immediately.

Maybe he forgot to tell me something, Jeremy thought as he picked up the receiver.

"Hello, Jeremy. I wanted you to know I kept my promise," Joan Bell said.

For a moment Jeremy's mind went blank, and he did not know what Joan meant. "How was Memphis?" he asked.

Joan's laugh was warm and rich. "The music was cool and the ribs. . . Well, come over for supper tonight and judge for yourself if they're as good as ever."

In the background Jeremy heard a shrill buzzer and knew she must have called him between classes. "You remembered. Thank you," he said, hoping his false heartiness would disguise his memory lapse.

"I'll take that as a 'yes.' Come about six-thirty. See you then."

Jeremy replaced the receiver and sat staring at the telephone for a long moment. He half-wished Joan had not invited him to her house again, but there was no way he could have refused to come without hurting her feelings. He could not afford to do that, especially now that it seemed he might need the Bells' help even sooner than he had anticipated.

"Are you all right?" Mr. Bell's voice roused Jeremy from his reverie, and he turned and nodded.

"Yes, sir. I was just thinking about the Schmidt girl's case."

"You can do that later. The hearing is still more than a week off, and there's a matter I'd like you to see to this morning if you're free."

"Certainly. Will I need my old clothes?"

"No, this doesn't involve a title search. Come into my office and I'll tell you about it."

Jeremy closed the Schmidt folder and pushed it to one side. For now, it would have to wait, but soon, very soon, he would talk to Toni, and April would be with her during the interview.

I won't forget about you.

That Jeremy's silent pledge was more to April Kincaid than to Toni Schmidt might be unprofessional, but at the moment, it was the way he felt.

seven

"Did you see who was at the service yesterday?" Tom Statum asked April when she came to work on Monday.

"A bunch of people," April replied. "Anybody in particular?" She had a good idea who Tom was talking about, but since she had not actually seen Jeremy in the congregation, she chose not to mention his name.

Tom looked disappointed. "Jeremy Winter was there. I thought maybe you noticed him, since you have legal business with him and all."

April had turned her back to put on her apron, and she was glad that Tom could not see the way her face warmed at the very mention of Jeremy's name. "No, I didn't see him. I don't see anyone when I'm singing," she added.

"That music was nice yesterday," Tom said. "I can't hardly wait to see what you and Ted will do for Easter services."

"Ted has big plans for the regular worship service, but whatever we do at the sunrise service will have to be simple."

"That's better, anyway, if you ask me. I reckon the Lord don't have to have fancy music, as along as it honors Him."

April tried not to think about Jeremy Winter as she went about her regular duties. Yet, knowing for sure that he had been there at the Community Church and had heard her sing made April vaguely uncomfortable. She sang as an act of worship and as a testimony to her Redeemer, not to impress anyone with her talent. Would Jeremy Winter understand? Many people insisted that April ought to "do something" with her vocal talent. When she replied that she felt she was doing what God wanted her to with His gift, many responded with doubt and disbelief.

"If I had a voice like yours, I sure wouldn't stay in Rockdale," Hoyt Greene had told her. April had gone out with him a few times, but after he had heard her sing, he pestered her about it so much that she had been glad when his company transferred him to Mobile.

As for Jeremy Winter, he had said he wanted her to be there when he interviewed Toni, so she should see him again soon, even if, as April suspected, Jeremy Winter never came back to the Community Church.

He's probably more comfortable at First Church, she thought.

❧

Jeremy spent Monday evening at the Bells' house, enjoying the barbecued ribs and all the fixings that went with them that Joan had brought back from Memphis.

After they ate, Randall Bell retreated to the den with his newspaper while Jeremy helped Joan clear away the dishes.

"Sit here at the kitchen table. I want to show you something," Joan said. She returned a moment later, pulled her chair close to Jeremy's, and opened her high school senior annual. She pointed out various Warrens, Bells, Westleighs, and Randalls. "About half the class are either your cousins or mine."

Jeremy looked at the unfamiliar faces and shook his head. "I never even heard of most of these people."

"You'll have a chance this summer when we have our tenth reunion. I'm in charge of the arrangements, and you can come and meet them. Lots of them will vote for you when you run for office."

Joan spoke so matter-of-factly that at first Jeremy wondered if he had heard her correctly. "What did you say?" he asked.

Her rich laugh told Jeremy that his astonishment had showed. "You don't have to pretend with me, Jeremy. Daddy told me you're planning to go into politics. When you do, you'll need all the support you can get."

She sounds like Guy Pettibone, Jeremy thought. *They'd make a great pair.* But neither Joan nor her father knew that he had hired a political consultant, nor had he specifically mentioned running for Harrison's seat in Congress. Although Joan had given him a perfect opening to tell her his plans, Jeremy felt strangely reluctant to do so.

"I appreciate what you and your father have done to help me already, when I'm practically a stranger—"

Before Jeremy could finish, Joan leaned forward and lightly brushed her lips against his. "Hush," she whispered.

Has she been wearing that perfume all night? Jeremy breathed in the warm scent and closed his eyes. He felt Joan's arms go around his neck, and the pressure of her lips increase. Almost involuntarily, Jeremy found himself returning the kiss. Then, recalling the look of glory on April's face when she sang, Jeremy pulled away.

Misunderstanding his reason for breaking off their kiss, Joan put her hand on Jeremy's cheek and spoke in a throaty whisper. "Daddy's watching TV. He's not paying us a bit of attention."

"It's not that—" Jeremy stopped when he realized he did not know what he could say that would explain why he did not want to kiss her.

Joan's eyes narrowed and she cocked her head to one side, assessing Jeremy as if she had never seen him before. "Daddy said you didn't have any. . .ties. If he's wrong and there's someone else—"

"No, it's not that" Jeremy said hastily. "But I don't want

to appear to be using you and your father just to further my own selfish ambitions."

Even as he spoke, Jeremy thought his explanation sounded stiff and unnatural, but Joan seemed to accept it at face value.

"You're entirely too noble for your own good," she murmured, and leaned toward him.

Sensing that Joan intended to kiss him again, Jeremy stood so abruptly that he almost overturned his chair. He tried to speak lightly. "You're wrong about that. But as much as I've enjoyed the evening, it's getting late, and we both have to work tomorrow."

Joan looked disappointed, but she did not try to persuade him to stay longer. "I'll see you to the door," she said after Jeremy went into the den and told her father goodbye.

"I think I can find it by myself," he said.

"Maybe so, but as a proper hostess, I can't let you take any risks."

Joan came outside with Jeremy, and he feared that she intended to follow him even farther. "I can find my car, too," he said, still keeping a light tone.

Joan glanced around as if to see if any of their neighbors might be watching, then took Jeremy's hand as if to shake it. "We must continue this discussion later."

Jeremy shook her hand, then immediately dropped it. "Thanks for bringing back the ribs. They were great."

"Any time. After all, a man deserves to have his ribs."

"Tell that to Adam," Jeremy said, surprised that the witticism had come so easily.

Joan's warm laughter followed him to the car, and even after he turned back for a final farewell wave, Jeremy felt that in some strange way, Joan still clung to him.

I'll have to do something about her, Jeremy thought, although he had no idea what.

Joan waved back, aware that it was too dark for him to see her quiet smile of triumph. Jeremy Winter might pretend to be half-afraid of her, she thought, but this time he had looked back. It was just a matter of time until she would have him eating out of her hand.

❧

It took Jeremy two days and many telephone calls to coordinate arrangements for Toni Schmidt to come to his office. Toni arrived there on Thursday afternoon, delivered by Evelyn Trent after Toni's foster mother said she did not have time to pick her up at Rockdale High School.

"She can walk. It won't hurt her," Mrs. Potter argued. However, the social worker had agreed with Jeremy that three miles was a bit too far for Toni to walk, especially since cloudy skies promised possible spring storms.

"Thanks for bringing her, Mrs. Trent. I'll see that Toni gets home."

The social worker's frosty expression told Jeremy she did not like his suggestion. "Not by yourself you won't," she said.

"Where's April?" Toni asked. "She can go with us."

Jeremy glanced at his watch. "I told her we'd meet at three-fifteen. I'm sure she'll be here any minute."

"I'll wait, then," Evelyn Trent said. However, she had just seated herself beside Toni when Edith Westleigh rapped on Jeremy's door, then opened it to admit April.

"Here she is now," Jeremy said unnecessarily. "Can you go with me to take Toni home when we're through here?"

April looked from Jeremy to Evelyn Trent and back again, obviously puzzled by the request. "Yes, as long as I get to work by five o'clock."

"I'm sure we'll be done by then if we start now."

Mrs. Trent stood and shrugged. "I can take a hint. I know when I'm not wanted."

Jeremy opened his office door for the social worker. "I suppose we'll see you in court. Thanks again for bringing Toni."

"I wondered why the social worker was here," April said when Jeremy returned to his desk and indicated for April to be seated.

"She had to bring me 'cause ol' Miz Prissy Potter's too busy," Toni said with heavy sarcasm.

"I hope you don't call her that to her face," April said.

"Of course not," Toni said impatiently, but it was obvious that she would like to.

"April's right," Jeremy told Toni. "Mrs. Potter will be called to testify concerning your current behavior. It wouldn't be smart to do anything to make her mad at you."

Toni lowered her head and sullenly picked at a hangnail. "I don't, but she hates me anyhow."

April took Toni's hand and spoke with quiet firmness. "I thought we had an agreement about that kind of talk."

"You don't have to live with the Potters," Toni protested.

In an attempt to stop what seemed to be a potential and fruitless argument, Jeremy cleared his throat. "Perhaps we should get started now," he said.

Toni's sullen expression, one that Jeremy had begun to think was habitual, did not change, but April looked relieved. "That's a good idea," she said.

&

An hour and fifteen minutes later, Jeremy had determined that Toni Schmidt would almost rather go to reform school than to have to stay on with the Potters, but under no circumstances would she ever want to live under the same roof as her stepmother. Toni's response about what she wanted to do—to stay on in Rockdale, with April as her guardian, until she graduated from high school—was equally emphatic.

"What will you do then?" Jeremy asked.

"Join the Marines," Toni said without hesitation.

Knowing that Toni seemed unable to joke about anything, Jeremy stifled his impulse to laugh. "You certainly don't want reform school on your record, then," he said.

April nodded. "That's what I keep telling Toni."

Jeremy glanced at his watch, then closed the file folder and replaced the cap on his pen. "I think we've done about all we can for now," he said. "It's time to take Toni home."

"It's no home to me," Toni muttered darkly, but neither April nor Jeremy responded to her statement, and the girl remained silent during the drive to the Potters.

"Turn right at the next intersection," April directed a few minutes later.

"I didn't realize the Potters lived so far out," Jeremy said when he finally reached a two-story frame house where several chickens scratched listlessly in an almost bare yard.

"Yeah, there's nothing like the country life," Toni said with her usual sarcasm.

"Toni, Toni, Toni!"

Several children came running out of the house and threw their arms around Toni's knees as soon as she got out of the car.

For a moment Toni's face softened, but she spoke to them roughly. "Hey, you guys, lay off!"

"Good-bye, Toni," April called to the girl's retreating back. "If you need anything, call me."

Without looking back at them, the girl raised one hand in a lazy wave.

Jeremy backed out of the driveway and glanced at April, whose eyes seemed unnaturally bright.

She's really cares about that bratty girl, Jeremy thought in wonder.

As if she sensed how Jeremy felt about Toni, April

defended the girl. "Toni tries to hide it, but she really likes those kids."

"Maybe that's because they like her, too," Jeremy said. "From what you tell me, not many people ever have."

April looked almost grateful. "That's true. You must understand that Toni isn't nearly as tough as she tries to act like she is. If she's sent to reform school. . ."

"Let's hope she won't be," Jeremy said when April seemed unable to finish the thought.

April looked doubtful. "Do you really think you can keep her from being sent away?"

"I'm going to try my hardest. But we need to talk about your being her guardian."

"Toni wants it and I'm willing. What's the problem?"

"The DHR, for one thing. Before they give up custody, they'll want to make sure you can handle the responsibility."

April raised her head in the way that Jeremy was coming to see as characteristic when she encountered something she did not like. "I won't have to do it by myself. Many people at my church have already promised to help."

Jeremy nodded. "I suppose you mean the Community Church?"

"You saw me there yesterday," April said, making it a statement.

"I wasn't sure you knew I was there," Jeremy said, a little disappointed that April had not made any effort to speak to him.

April hesitated, then decided to tell the truth. "I didn't until I saw someone who looked like you leave the parking lot in a big hurry. Later, Mr. Statum told me that your folks had built the original building."

"That was a long time ago." Neither spoke as Jeremy pulled away from a traffic light and stopped in front of Statum's Family Restaurant. He shut off the motor and turned toward April. "You didn't tell me you could sing," he said.

April already had her hand on the door handle, but she turned around and stared at Jeremy. "When was I supposed to do that?" she asked.

Then, leaving Jeremy to stare after her open-mouthed, April got out of the car and hurried into the restaurant just as the clock atop the Rock County Courthouse struck five times, and with a loud clap of thunder, a deluge of rain fell.

Jeremy realized he had upset April by speaking of her singing. It was too late to go after her now, but he could come back later.

It's time I had supper at Statum's again, anyway. I'm tired of my own cooking, Jeremy told himself.

When Jeremy returned to the office for a file he wanted to review, he was surprised to find Randall Bell still there. He came into Jeremy's office and sat down as if he intended to stay a while.

"Guy Pettibone called," he said.

Jeremy had never mentioned his name, but from Randall Bell's expression, Jeremy was certain that he knew who Guy Pettibone was and exactly what he did for a living.

"Did he say I should call him?" Jeremy asked.

Mr. Bell nodded. "Among other things. Your uncle told me you had some political ambitions, but I had no idea that you were this serious about them."

Jeremy tried to ignore the implied criticism in Mr. Bell's tone and made his own reply more statement than an apology. "I was taught to believe that anything worth doing at all is worth doing well."

"Guy Pettibone is the best at what he does, all right. You did well to consult him, but you should have told me about it from the first. He was surprised that I didn't know your plans."

Jeremy felt faintly uneasy. "I would have told you when

the time came," he said, then added, "You two must have had a long conversation."

Randall Bell shrugged. "Long enough. The gist of it is I agreed to get in touch with my Montgomery contacts and see what might happen when Harrison resigns."

"I see. That's very kind of you." Jeremy tried not to sound as dismayed as he felt. He knew he needed Randall Bell's help, but he did not want the older man to take charge of his life—and he feared that that might be about to happen.

"Not at all. When I told Joan you might run for office, right away she said she wants to help you. I'm glad that you two are getting along so well. Men have had a way of disappointing my daughter. It's about time Joan found someone worthy of her trust."

Jeremy swallowed hard and searched for the right words. "Your daughter is a wonderful person, and you've both been more than kind to me," he said as impersonally as he could. "You should know how much I appreciate it."

"Umm." Mr. Bell steepled his fingers and looked appraisingly at Jeremy. "I've always thought that actions speak louder than words. You're being watched, Jeremy, by more people than you know. Be careful what you do."

It was not the first time Jeremy had heard such advice, and he did not have to ask Mr. Bell what he meant for he knew all too well. "Yes, sir. I don't think you have anything to worry about."

Randall Bell stood and glanced at his watch. "Well, in any case I'm not the one who wants to run for Congress. Mr. Pettibone said for you to call him."

"Yes, I'll do that. Thanks."

Jeremy waited until he heard Randall Bell leave the building, then he let out his breath in a long sigh before he punched in Guy Pettibone's beeper number.

❧

Not long before closing time that evening, April was in the

kitchen when she heard Tom Statum greet someone warmly. She looked out and saw him shaking Jeremy Winter's hand. "Have a seat. April will be with you in a minute," she heard Tom say.

April emerged from the kitchen, picked up a menu, and arrived at Jeremy's booth just as he slid into it.

"See, I told you," Tom said. "How's that for fast service?"

"Great. It beats eating at home alone, anyway."

"That's what all our reg'lars say," Tom declared. "Only thing is, you ought to come in earlier. By this time, we're usually out of some of the daily specials."

"I'll keep that in mind," Jeremy said.

"I thought maybe you didn't like the food here," April said when Tom left and went over to the cash register to take a diner's check.

"Not at all. I eat at home most of the time, but I'm afraid I'm not much of a cook," Jeremy said.

April had to struggle to keep her usual friendly waitress smile from revealing her true feelings. "I'll get your water and be back in a minute to take your order," she said.

When April went behind the counter to the ice machine, Tom Statum joined her. "You oughter go out of your way to be nice to that young man. He could use a friend."

April looked at Tom in surprise. "What makes you say that?"

"Never mind. Just remember what I said."

When April returned to the table with the water, Jeremy handed her the menu even before she could ask what he wanted to order. "I'll take whatever you recommend."

"Everyone says the baked chicken and dressing is good. It comes with green beans and sweet potatoes. I think there's enough left for at least one more serving."

Jeremy nodded. "Then I'll have it."

April started to leave, then turned back to ask another question. "Roll or corn bread?" she asked.

"I thought corn bread came with all the plates," Jeremy said. "At least, that's what you gave me when I was here before."

He remembers that? April thought. "You have a choice," she said aloud.

"Then make it corn bread."

"All right." April nodded and started to turn away until Jeremy reached out a detaining hand.

"There's one more thing, April."

The tone of his voice and the touch of his hand were unsettling, but April made herself look at Jeremy and spoke in a firm voice. "Yes? What is it?"

"When you're through here tonight, can I take you home?"

April felt as if the breath had been knocked from her body, so unexpected was his request. *Oh, yes, Jeremy, I'll be glad to have you take me home,* she wanted to say. But her natural reserve would never allow her to speak so frankly. "If it's about Toni. . . ," she began, but he shook his head.

"No, this has nothing to do with her," he said.

April glanced back at Tom. "Mr. Statum usually takes me home when it's raining."

"Tell him you already have a ride."

April nodded. "All right." Then she withdrew her hand from Jeremy's. "Your order will be ready in a few minutes," she added in her best professional waitress tone.

But back in the kitchen, April felt far from professional, and even the cook noticed her expression.

"You look mighty happy, Miss April. Somebody musta give you a mighty big tip."

"Something like that," April said.

Something better than that, she thought. *Dear Lord, don't let me feel this way about Jeremy Winter unless something good can come of it.*

eight

Jeremy, accustomed to dining alone and in haste and often scarcely heeding what he ate, made himself slow the process as much as he could, until finally he was Statum's Family Restaurant's last remaining diner.

At five minutes until nine Tom Statum reversed the "Open" sign and locked the door. "I'll finish up. You can leave whenever you're ready."

April glanced at Jeremy. "Can I get you anything else?"

"No, thanks."

April nodded and went into the kitchen, Jeremy supposed to take off her apron, and he stood and reached for his wallet.

"How was everything?" Tom asked at the cash register.

"Very good," Jeremy said, although in truth he had paid far more attention to April than to what she had served him.

Tom handed Jeremy his change, then leaned forward slightly and spoke with a lowered voice. "That April's one fine girl. She could use a friend like you about now."

Not knowing quite what to say, Jeremy merely nodded. April came out of the kitchen and told Tom good night, then walked to the front door and opened it with her key before Jeremy could offer to do it for her.

"See you later," Tom called after them as Jeremy and April went outside.

It occurred to Jeremy that he and April were alone together after dark for the first time, and he wondered if that was why she seemed so uneasy. "My car is over there across the street." Jeremy opened the passenger door for April, then took his seat behind the wheel and inserted the key into the ignition without starting the engine. "Is there some place else you'd like to go?"

April's laugh was barely audible. "In Rockdale at this hour, there's only Scooter's."

Jeremy recalled the road house's unsavory reputation. "I'm sure that's not the kind of place either of us needs to be seen," he said.

"Just take me home." April sounded so tense that Jeremy feared he had somehow offended her.

"I don't know where you live," he said.

"Fifteen twenty Harrison," April said. "It's near Dale Boulevard."

With a jolt Jeremy realized that April's apartment, which Toni had broken into, was located in Rockdale's only low-rent housing complex. Harrison Homes had been so named for the Congressman who had helped get it built and whom Jeremy now wanted to replace in Washington.

Small world, he thought. Jeremy would have said so to Joan Bell, but April knew nothing about his political ambitions, and for now, it seemed better to leave it that way.

"This whole area was an eyesore for years," Jeremy said. "The housing project is one of the best things that Harrison ever did."

"Harrison?" April's tone made it clear that she did not know who he was.

"The congressman from this district. The project wouldn't have been built without his help."

"Turn here. It's the last unit on the right," April said.

Jeremy shut off the ignition and surveyed the one-story brick apartment, distinguished from its neighbors by the small grapevine wreath studded with dried flowers on the front door.

"The place looks nice," Jeremy commented.

April sighed. "It's still public housing." Then she turned to Jeremy and spoke with anxiety in her voice. "Will living here hurt my chances to become Toni's guardian? Because if so, I've been saving up. I should have enough for a deposit on a better place."

Jeremy wanted to take April's hands, now clasped together under her chin in an attitude of supplication, and reassure her that it did not matter, but he could not give her any false hopes. "That's just part of it," he said. "You don't have a car, and that's a disadvantage," Jeremy said.

"Tom Statum's looking for a used car I can afford. In the meantime, he or Tim Brown take me wherever I can't ride my bike."

"I hope he finds something for you soon," Jeremy said.

April looked around uneasily. "We should go inside," she said. "Someone's likely to offer you a hit if you stay in the car."

"A hit?" Jeremy repeated. Although he knew quite well that April referred to a drug deal, Jeremy was surprised to think that such things could happen in a quiet place like Rockdale, and he said so.

"I'm afraid there aren't many safe places left anymore," April said with a note of sadness.

"It sounds like you speak from experience," Jeremy said.

When April quickly opened her door and got out of the car, Jeremy guessed it was in part because she did not want to talk about her past, whatever it might have been.

Jeremy followed April into the apartment and waited at the door while she switched on a table lamp and illuminated a clean and neat but very sparsely furnished room. From his vantage point just inside the front door, Jeremy could see all of the apartment's rooms. A small kitchen opened to the left of the living room, with a bedroom and bath visible to the rear. Two mountain bikes leaned against the apartment's front wall.

"You have two bikes?" he asked April.

"I keep one here for when Toni visits. She likes to ride, too."

I'd feel cramped in this place, even by myself, Jeremy thought. "Do you really have enough room for Toni?" he asked aloud.

April looked surprised at his question. "Of course," she said. "The couch makes into a bed, and Toni doesn't need much space. You should see where she has to stay at the Potters' house."

"Foster homes aren't usually luxurious," Jeremy said, "but from what Toni says, she'd rather stay in one than go to reform school."

April started to speak, then seemed to remember her role as hostess. "Please, sit down. Would you like a cup of coffee?"

"Thanks. That sounds good," Jeremy said.

A few minutes later, when April brought out a tray set with two cheap stoneware mugs and a couple of slices of homemade coffee cake on a chipped plate, Jeremy could not help comparing her and Joan Bell as hostesses. Both had tried to make Jeremy comfortable and had given him the best they had to offer. April's apartment lacked the expensive furnishings and fine china of the Bells' home, but somehow Jeremy felt more comfortable in it.

"This is delicious. When do you have time to bake?" Jeremy asked.

His praise seemed to embarrass April. "I enjoy it. Toni

wants to learn how to 'cook fancy,' as she puts it. There's lots of things like that we could do together."

Jeremy nodded. "I'm sure that's so, but if you don't mind, I'd rather not talk about Toni tonight."

April seemed momentarily flustered. "Can I get you more coffee?" she asked.

"Yes, thanks. It's good." Jeremy noticed that April's hand, which no doubt effortlessly poured dozens of refills each day, shook slightly as she refilled his cup. *I'm making her uncomfortable,* he realized, and decided to make his apology.

"I didn't mean to upset you when I said what I did about your singing. It was stupid of me. Of course you don't go around telling strangers that you have a gorgeous voice. I was trying to pay you a sincere compliment, and if I seemed out of line, please forgive me."

In contrast to his usual well-thought-out speeches, Jeremy spoke in a rush, and when April lowered her head as if she could not stand to look at him, Jeremy thought he had made matters even worse, and added, "Okay?"

April nodded her head, then raised it and looked at Jeremy in a way that made his heart seem to skip a beat. "I've never had many compliments, so I don't rightly know how to take them," April said. "I don't sing anywhere except church," she added, her tone suggesting that he might try to argue the point.

"God has given you a wonderful talent," Jeremy said sincerely. "I don't blame you for wanting to use it for Him."

April's eyes widened slightly. "I didn't expect. . .I mean, you don't have to apologize to me for anything," she said.

"Good. No matter what happens with Toni's hearing, I hope we can still be friends."

"So do I," April said.

Jeremy glanced at his watch and stood. "I'd better go now. I'll see you at the hearing?"

"Yes, but we're having a sunrise service on Warren Mountain Sunday morning. You're welcome to come."

I want you to be there, her eyes told him, and Jeremy smiled.

"All right. I'll try to make it," Jeremy said. "Thanks for the coffee."

April walked to the door ahead of Jeremy and opened it for him. "Good night," she said.

"You, too." Jeremy lingered at the door, aware that he did not really want to leave. He wanted to cradle April's face in his hands and kiss her.

Instead, he took her hand in his and held it. Their eyes met, and Jeremy hoped that the intensity of his gaze would speak for him before he released April's hand and turned away.

"Stay safe," April said, so faintly that Jeremy was not sure whether he had really heard her, or had merely thought the words that his grandmother had said to him so often over the years.

You stay safe, too, sweet April. By the time Jeremy could turn back to give voice to the words, April had closed her door.

Thinking April just might be watching him, Jeremy waved once more before he turned back and got into his car.

❧

The next day, Jeremy walked into the office to the sound of his ringing telephone and picked up the receiver to hear Guy Pettibone's secretary say that he had been trying to reach him. "I'll put him through now, Mr. Winter," she said.

"I called your beeper number yesterday," Jeremy said

when Mr. Pettibone came on the line. "I'm sorry I missed you."

"Big things underfoot, boy. The word is that the governor's calling a meeting in Montgomery next week to discuss what to do about Harrison's seat. Nothing public yet, but all the movers and shakers will be there, and so should you."

"I haven't been invited," Jeremy said.

Guy Pettibone snorted. "Boy, don't you know that line about the timid heart never won the fair lady? Randall Bell will be there. Just make sure that you go with him."

Jeremy felt a bit dazed. He sank down into his chair and swallowed hard. *I seem to be losing control of my life to Guy Pettibone and Randall Bell,* he thought. "When did he tell you that?" he asked.

"Last night. When I couldn't get you at home, I called him. Bell's a good man, and he knows the right people. But you really a beeper. A cellular phone's no good if you don't answer it."

Jeremy tried hard not to sound defensive. "I'm sorry I missed your call. I ate out and didn't get home until late. Mr. Bell can fill me in on the Montgomery meeting."

"Yes, but in the meantime I've put out some other feelers that he doesn't know about. Bell's going strictly with his party, and you don't want a party label just yet. Someone without that baggage might just slip right in while the good ole boys are still fighting each other, doing business the old way."

"So I shouldn't commit to anything yet?"

"Nothing except getting your name and face known. Go on to Montgomery, but don't let on like you even recognize Harrison's name. You understand what I'm telling you, boy?"

Although Mr. Pettibone always managed to make Jeremy feel about ten years old, he cleared his throat and tried to sound sure of himself. "Yes, sir, I understand. Shall I call you when we get back?"

"Yes, or even sooner if anything changes. What's decided in the next few weeks will be critical. Stay on top of it, you hear?"

"Yes, I'll do that."

As usual, Guy Pettibone hung up the telephone almost before Jeremy could say good-bye. *Mr. Pettibone's not a man to waste words,* he thought.

Then Jeremy heard Randall Bell speaking to Edith, and he wondered what the two men had said about him. *I should hear Mr. Bell's version in about ten seconds,* he thought, but it actually took the older lawyer no more than seven seconds to rap lightly on Jeremy's office door.

"Hello, there, Jeremy," he said. "Where did you get to last night? That Pettibone man was fit to be tied when he couldn't get hold of you."

"I went out to eat, but there weren't any messages on my machine when I got home."

"I suppose he doesn't like those contraptions any better than I do," Randall Bell said. "Anyhow, we had a nice talk about your chances for Harrison's seat. He thinks you ought to go to Montgomery with me next week."

Jeremy nodded. "I know. . .I just talked to him. What day is this meeting?"

"I'm not sure yet, but except for the Miller deposition on Monday and the Schmidt hearing, your calendar looks clear. We can probably postpone the Schmidt thing."

Jeremy thought of how disappointed both April and Toni would be if her hearing were further delayed. "I hope that won't be necessary," he said.

Randall Bell raised a questioning eyebrow. "That's small potatoes compared to what's happening in Montgomery. You won't ever get anywhere if you let small-town cases tie you up."

"You seem to like it here well enough," Jeremy dared to say.

Mr. Bell looked thoughtful. "I'll grant you that there's a lot to be said about being a big frog in a little pond, but if I had it to do all over again with the advantages you have . . .well, I just might be Senator Bell right now."

That Randall Bell might have had his own political ambitions had not occurred to Jeremy. "What happened that you didn't try for it?"

Mr. Bell shrugged. "Several things, including Joan's mother. She made it clear that she wanted no part of politics, and if I did, I'd have to do it on my own."

"Which means in those days you couldn't do it at all," Jeremy said, understanding Mr. Bell's dilemma.

"Those days or these, it's all the same. A man who wants to run for anything, from dogcatcher right on up the line, needs his wife's support. Without it, he hasn't much chance."

He sounds like Mr. Pettibone, Jeremy thought with some discomfort. *The next thing I know, Mr. Bell will be telling me how lucky I am to have a woman like his daughter to help me campaign.*

"It's not too late," Jeremy pointed out. "You're hardly dead with old age, and I'm sure your daughter would be a great help to you."

Randall Bell laughed ruefully. "I'm afraid too much water's already passed under that bridge for me. But you're right about Joan. She's not at all like her mother. When it comes to politics, Joan likes a good fight. You'll see."

Jeremy was saved from having to comment on that when Edith came to the office door to say that Evelyn Trent, Toni Schmidt's social worker, wanted to make an appointment to see him.

"The DHR office is closed for Good Friday, but she says she's willing to come in on her own time," Edith added.

Good Friday. April had invited him to come to the Easter sunrise service, so Jeremy should have realized what this day was.

"Tell her I can see her at ten o'clock," Jeremy said.

"We'll close the office at noon ourselves," Randall Bell said when Edith withdrew. "Hardly anybody stirs from noon on."

"Will there be special church services?" Jeremy asked.

"Not at First Church. Some of the others do something, I think, but most people stay home and rest up for Easter. That's the big day. First puts on quite a show. I think you'll enjoy it."

A church service shouldn't be a show. Jeremy would have said so, but he had learned that a political aspirant never talked about the specifics of his religion. It was good to be seen attending a solid, "mainstream" church, but not to talk about it too much.

"Will there be a sunrise service?" Jeremy asked.

If he had asked if the aisles would be turned into bowling lanes, Mr. Bell could hardly have looked more shocked. "Of course not," he said, "but there'll be a big crowd at the regular service. You have to come early to get a place to park."

"I'll keep that in mind," Jeremy said.

"I've a few files to go over, then I'll be leaving. If I don't see you again before then, Joan said to tell you she hopes you'll join us at the Country Club for brunch after church."

"Thanks, but I'm not sure of my Sunday plans," Jeremy heard himself saying.

"Then you can call Joan and tell her that yourself. She'll think I didn't ask you nicely enough."

I don't want to call Joan Bell, today or any other day, was Jeremy's first thought, but he knew that that was not entirely true. His political career needed a woman like Joan Bell, and he was extremely fortunate to have her on his side. Only a reckless fool would totally disregard her.

"I'll do that," Jeremy promised.

When Randall Bell left, Jeremy turned his attention to Toni Schmidt's case. What was Evelyn Trent's concern, coming to see him on her day off?

Whatever it is, I doubt if it means anything good for Toni, Jeremy thought as he opened the file and referred once more to the social worker's notes.

&

In her twenty-five years with the DHR, Evelyn Trent had seen it all, from child abuse to welfare fraud and everything in between. She took pride in her ability to keep her emotions out of her work and seldom did anything that was not strictly according to the book. But Toni Schmidt's case was different, and she did not like the way it had been going ever since Randall Bell turned it over to his young associate.

"Thank you for seeing me on such short notice," Evelyn Trent said when Jeremy invited her to have a seat. "I'm sure you want to quit work early today, so I'll make this brief."

"I'm in no hurry, Mrs. Trent. What seems to be the problem?"

Evelyn Trent's fair face flushed slightly. "I don't have a problem but you will if you go to court and petition for

April Kincaid to be Toni's guardian."

Even though he was caught off guard, Jeremy tried not to show it. "How did you know about that?"

"Toni took great pleasure in telling me that soon she wouldn't have to do what we tell her to, because April is going to be her guardian. Is that what you intend?"

That wasn't very smart of Toni, Jeremy thought, but he masked his concern with a shrug. "I haven't decided yet," he said. "Would DHR object to that?"

The social worker nodded vigorously. "We certainly would. Toni needs a more mature and stable influence than a young woman like April Kincaid."

"Miss Kincaid seems to be both mature and stable," Jeremy said.

Evelyn Trent pursed her lips. "How much do you know about her past?"

"Evidently not as much as you seem to," Jeremy said, the need to defend April momentarily overriding his professional judgment. "Perhaps you'll enlighten me?"

"I don't repeat gossip and hearsay," Evelyn Trent said somewhat stiffly. "I'm merely suggesting that you ask the court to let Toni stay with the Potters."

"The DHR would have no objection to that?" he asked.

"We would go along with it on a continuing probationary basis. Should Toni get out of line again, we'd again petition for her to be remanded to the custody of the State."

In other words, Toni would be summarily shipped off to reform school. Jeremy did not have to say the words aloud; he knew Mrs. Trent was quite aware of the possible consequences.

"I'll consider what you've said, and I appreciate your concern," Jeremy said.

Mrs. Trent stood and nodded her head briefly. "I'm sure

you do. I've had my say, the rest is up to you."

"Thank you for coming in," Jeremy said with studied politeness. "I suppose I'll see you in court next week?"

"I wouldn't miss it for the world," Miss Trent said with a hint of sarcasm.

Neither would I, Jeremy thought. There was no way he could ask for a postponement now. The longer Evelyn Trent had to spread doubts about April, the more difficult it would be to keep Toni in Rockdale, with or without April's being her guardian.

"Have a happy Easter," Mrs. Trent said over her shoulder as she left his office.

"You, too," Jeremy responded automatically. But Evelyn Trent's mention reminded him that he had been invited to the Community Church's Easter sunrise service.

I won't have far to go. It's on Warren Mountain, Jeremy thought. April Kincaid would be there, and he could hear her sing.

"I'll be there, for sure," Jeremy said aloud.

nine

Warren Mountain had never completely belonged to the Warrens, but since they had been the first to build on its flat ridges and gentle slopes, their name had been given to the entire range that stretched for several miles in a generally south-southwesterly direction. A natural amphitheater had been cut from the rock on the peak just beyond the Warren family cemetery, and it was there, where the sun's first rays touched the land, that sunrise services were traditionally held.

Jeremy could have walked up the mountain, even in the predawn darkness, but he drove so he could offer to take April home afterward. From the number of cars that had already passed the house before he left, Jeremy correctly guessed that the informal parking area at the base of the amphitheater would be crowded. He backed into a space in the grass and followed a large, mostly silent crowd up the hill. At first it was hard to make out faces in the chill grayness, but as the time of sunrise grew closer, Jeremy recognized a few people, including Tom Statum. April was nowhere in sight, however, nor were the pastor and the song leader.

They're probably waiting to make a grand entrance, Jeremy thought.

As one, every face turned toward the top of the peak at their right, where a bright glow announced the arrival of the sun. At the very moment that its first beams penetrated the grayness, three women in long robes walked out of the woods and stopped before a low structure that had been built to represent Christ's tomb. Within it, another figure, dressed in white, was barely visible.

"Where is our Master?" asked one of the women.

"What have ye done with Him?" said another.

" 'Be not affrighted: Ye seek Jesus of Nazareth, which was crucified: he is risen; he is not here: behold the place where they laid him. But go your way, tell his disciples and Peter that he goeth before you into Galilee: there shall ye see him, as he said unto you.' "*

The women turned and went back in the direction from which they had come, and Jeremy felt his scalp prickle as April stepped out from behind the representation of the tomb and the first triumphant notes of a familiar Easter hymn by Charles Wesley soared into the dawn.

> *Christ the Lord is risen today,*
> *Al—le-lu-ia!*
> *Sons of men and angels say,*
> *Al—le-lu-ia!*
> *Raise your joys and triumphs high,*
> *Al—le-lu-ia!*
> *Sing, ye heavens, and earth reply.*
> *Al—le-lu-ia!*

At the end of the first verse, the song leader joined April and motioned for everyone to sing. When the hymn ended, April took a seat in the front row, and the service proceeded with prayers, a short sermon, and more joint singing. The fully risen sun was bathing them all in its light when April stood once more.

Slowly she walked to stand before the representation of the empty tomb, raised her radiant face to the sun, closed her eyes, and began to sing, unaccompanied.

*Mark 16:6-7

"I know that my Redeemer liveth," she began.

A murmur of appreciation swept through the congregation, and even those who might not recognize Handel's soaring melody knew they were hearing something special on this, the most important day in the Christian calendar.

If it weren't for Easter, there wouldn't be any Christians. Jeremy could not recall the first time he had heard that, but he had long since accepted it as truth. If Christ had not risen from the dead, then He would be remembered, if at all, as another in the long line of prophets who brought their messages to a sinful world, then died and were buried and forgotten.

But as the words of April's song declared, Jesus, Who took on all sins for the sake of the world His Father had created, did rise from the dead, to live forevermore and to bring eternal life to all who believed in Him.

"Amen!" Jeremy heard himself saying with the others when the last long, true note faded away into the morning.

The service quickly concluded with another prayer and a praise chorus, then as silently as they had come, as if still under the spell of the joyful solemnity of the occasion, the worshipers began to leave.

Jeremy caught up with April and the red-haired music leader at the parking area and spoke softly to April. "Can I take you home?"

April looked at Jeremy almost blankly, as if struggling to recall who he was, then she nodded. "Yes. . .thanks," she said, almost in a whisper.

Silently Jeremy took April's hand and led her to his car, and even after they started down the mountain, neither spoke. But when Jeremy left the procession of cars and turned into his own driveway, April looked at him in surprise.

"This isn't where I live," she said.

"I offered to take you home. I just didn't say whose."

"I've often wondered what this place looked like on the inside," April said when they got out of the car. "It's such a pretty old house."

"Old, anyway. After I get it painted, it'll look a lot better. Come inside and I'll make us some breakfast," Jeremy added.

April looked uncertain if she should accept his invitation. "I could have fed you at my place," she said.

"Then I'll let you do the cooking," Jeremy said. "I usually just have those toaster pastry things."

April wrinkled her nose and shook her head. "If you can handle the coffee, I'll see what I can find."

A few minutes later, as they ate in companionable silence, Jeremy thought that April's cinnamon toast and omelet made the most wonderful breakfast he had had in years. And certainly having April sitting across from him at the old, green-painted kitchen table did not hurt, either.

"You make good coffee," April said after a while.

"And this is a mean omelet, lady," Jeremy replied. "Seems like you can cook about as good as you sing."

April's cheeks pinkened briefly, and she rose abruptly and carried her plate to the sink as if embarrassed by Jeremy's praise.

He followed her and got out the dishpan and put it in the sink. "I'll wash and you can dry," he said, but she shook her head.

"No. You know where things go and I don't. I'll wash and you can dry."

That's the way Joan did it, too. Jeremy wondered what had made him think of that.

"Evelyn Trent came to see me Friday," Jeremy said after

a moment. April's shoulders stiffened, but when she said nothing, Jeremy continued. "Apparently Toni told her you wanted to be her guardian."

April groaned. "Oh, no! I thought Toni knew better than to talk to Mrs. Trent about anything. What else did she say?"

Jeremy wiped a dish thoroughly and put it into the cabinet before he turned back and looked into April's eyes. "She says the DHR's willing to let Toni stay with the Potters, but not with you. She hinted that there would be trouble if we petitioned for you to be her guardian."

April lowered her eyes and, with studied diligence, resumed washing the dishes. "Did she say why?" she asked after a moment.

"She thinks you're too young and not stable enough."

Jeremy thought he detected a note of relief in April's voice. "Is that all?" Then she turned to face him. "Is that what you think?"

Almost automatically, Jeremy's arms went out to circle April's waist. "This is what I think," he said, then pulled her close and kissed her.

After a soft cry of surprise, April brought her hands out of the dishwater long enough to lay them lightly on Jeremy's shoulders. At first she answered his kiss with a light pressure, then she pulled away, picked up a dish towel, and dabbed at his shirt in the place where her hands had rested only a moment before.

"I'm afraid I got your shirt wet," she said.

"I don't mind." Jeremy caught April's hands in his and bent down to kiss her again. She did not resist, but when he would have deepened and prolonged the contact, she once more pulled away.

"Take me home now," April said levelly.

Jeremy matched her tone. "Of course." He did not attempt to apologize for kissing her. Although as a lawyer he knew he should not become involved with a client, Jeremy had enjoyed kissing April too much to pretend he had been wrong to do it.

April said nothing on the drive to her apartment, and when they reached her door, she turned and offered her hand to Jeremy. "I'm glad you came to the service this morning. . .and thanks for the breakfast."

"Thank you for inviting me. It was really special." *And so are you,* Jeremy wanted to say, and hoped that his eyes spoke for him. "And thanks for making breakfast. I liked that cinnamon toast."

"Now you know how it's done, anyway." April hesitated a moment, then looked down at the key in her hand as if it might hold the answer to some important question. Without looking at Jeremy, she spoke in a low voice. "About the hearing. . . If DHR doesn't want me to be Toni's guardian, I'd rather withdraw my petition."

"You don't have to do that—" Jeremy began, but April's stricken look silenced him.

"I think I do," she said quietly. "But I'd rather tell Toni myself."

Jeremy nodded. "All right. But—"

April looked at her watch and gasped. "I didn't realize the time. We still have another service today. So long, Jeremy."

April let herself into her apartment and Jeremy glanced at his own watch as he walked back to his car. He could still make the First Church service. The Bells were expecting him, and it would be a good time to put in another appearance at First Church. After all, many people would be there today that would not come to church again until next Easter. . .people whose votes he might soon need.

With that thought Jeremy started the car and left without looking back at the window where April stood, watching him.

❧

The first thing that Jeremy noticed when he entered the First Church sanctuary was the almost overpowering scent of lilies, which seemed to be everywhere. His nose twitched and his eyes watered, and Jeremy wondered briefly if he might be allergic to lilies. The second thing he noticed—Joan Bell in her new finery—soon made him forget the first. Jeremy searched for a name for the shade she was wearing; pale lavender or was it mauve? The dress was of some soft, flowing stuff, topped by a hat of the same material and adorned with what looked at first glance to be real spring flowers.

"They're silk," Joan explained when she saw Jeremy's puzzled expression.

"I'm glad you're here," Randall Bell said when Jeremy sat down between him and Joan. "I have some news about Montgomery."

"Oh? What's happening?" Jeremy asked, but with the first notes of the organ, Mr. Bell shook his head and put his index finger to his mouth.

"I'll tell you later," he said.

Jeremy nodded as the service began with the rather spectacular entrance of the choir coming down the center aisle, singing the same hymn that April had sung earlier.

First Church does put on a good Easter show, Jeremy had to admit as the service progressed. *But it can't hold a candle to what took place earlier on Warren Mountain.*

As he had done before, the First Church minister delivered a short sermon, and even with all the extra singing and what Jeremy called "parading around," the service still ended almost on the stroke of twelve. Again Jeremy was greeted by and in turn greeted many people who seemed gratified that he had remembered their names. So many stopped to talk to Jeremy that he and the Bells were almost the last to reach the church parking lot.

"Daddy, you can go on. I'll ride with Jeremy," Joan announced at the last minute.

"Jeremy and I have things to discuss," her father said.

"You can do that any time," Joan said breezily. "It is all right if I ride with you, isn't it?" she asked Jeremy, somewhat tardily.

"Of course," he said, and hastened to unlock and open the passenger door for her.

"You lock your car even at church?" Joan asked when Jeremy slid in behind the wheel.

"I lock it everywhere. . .force of habit," he replied. "You never know when someone might take a notion to steal it."

"Daddy says if thieves want a car they'll take it, and it's too much trouble to lock it all the time," Joan said. "Besides, you're not in Birmingham now. Rockdale doesn't have a problem with car thieves."

Joan Bell continued to chatter about how safe Rockdale was, and once again Jeremy was keenly aware of the subtle scent of her perfume, which seemed to be everywhere and nowhere, all at the same time. If April Kincaid wore perfume he was not aware of it, yet she always smelled sweet and fresh.

I mustn't keep trying to compare Joan and April, Jeremy told himself, but at every turn he found himself doing just that.

"Have you heard a word I've said?" Joan demanded when they reached the Country Club.

"Certainly," Jeremy replied. "The gist of it all is that

Rockdale is a wonderful place to raise a family."

Jeremy did not realize the effect of what he had said until Joan's face turned red and she got out of the car without waiting for him to assist her. *If I say anything else, I'll only make matters worse,* he thought. Instead, Jeremy took Joan's arm and escorted her into the Country Club, aware that many eyes followed their progress with interest.

"Don't they make a lovely couple?" the dowager, Minnie Reed, whispered to her longtime friend, Estelle Johnson, as they passed their table.

"That's a wedding just waiting to happen," Estelle said in a stage whisper that reached not only Jeremy and Joan, but just about everyone else in the dining room.

Neither Jeremy nor Joan made any reference to what they had overheard, but Jeremy had to agree with the first part. No matter what else anyone might say about them, he and Joan did, indeed, look good together.

Despite his earlier mention of news from Montgomery, Randall Bell waited until Joan had left the table after lunch before he told Jeremy what was happening.

"Due to the holiday weekend, hardly anyone's left in Montgomery, but my contacts tell me that the meeting to discuss Harrison's replacement is expected to take place later on this week. Keep your calendar clear so we can go down there when something breaks."

Jeremy's first reaction was relief. "That's good. I won't have to postpone the Schmidt hearing, after all," he said.

Randall Bell shook his head slightly. "You really are involved in that case, aren't you?"

"It's different from anything I've ever done before," Jeremy said, but he suspected that Mr. Bell knew there was more to it than that.

"Well, for the firm's sake I hope you win, but don't be

too surprised if it should go the other way."

Jeremy looked at Mr. Bell in surprise. "What makes you say that? If you know something that I don't—"

"I know the way this town works," he interrupted. "It doesn't know what to do with incorrigible juveniles."

Before Jeremy could protest that Toni was hardly incorrigible, Joan returned to the table, effectively closing the subject.

"It's such a lovely day, I think we ought to go somewhere," Joan said.

"Seems more like a good afternoon to rest and get caught up on some reading," Randall Bell said. "You two go on and do what you like," he added.

Joan smiled at Jeremy. "How about it? Are you game?"

"That depends. What do you have in mind?"

"I haven't hiked in a while. I thought we might explore your mountain."

"If you mean Warren Mountain, it's not mine," Jeremy said.

"Part of it is, though, and with the redbuds and dogwoods in bloom, it ought to be spectacular."

"I suppose so," said Jeremy, who had only vaguely noted the pale green, interspersed with white and pink, that now formed a backdrop on the hills behind his house.

Joan laughed, a rich sound that Jeremy still found appealing. "Don't sound so enthusiastic. You lawyer types tend to stay inside too much. A little fresh air will do you good."

"Surely you can't refuse such a flattering invitation," Randall Bell said wryly.

"Oh, I'm not," Jeremy said. He had no real reason to turn down Joan's suggestion, and in any case, to do so would be quite rude.

"Good. I'll come to your place in an hour or so, then."

⁊

April had made plans to spend Easter with Toni, beginning when the Potters brought the girl to the regular Community Church service on their way to their own place of worship.

"I feel like a dork in this dress," Toni muttered to April, who had given her the simple challis print the week before.

"You don't look like one, though," April assured her. "You should wear it to the hearing. It makes you look a lot older."

Toni brightened perceptibly. "Yeah? If I look old enough, maybe the judge will let me do what I want."

"Nobody ever gets that old," April said. "Come on and sit down. Our song is near the first."

"I don't know about this," Toni said. "Suppose I mess up?"

"You won't. We've practiced it enough to be perfect."

"Yeah, but that was just the two of us. In front of all of these people. . ."

"Close your eyes and they'll go away," April said. "That's what I always do. Hurry, put your bag down there by the umbrella stand and let's get inside."

When the time came, April took Toni's hand and led her to stand before the altar to sing "The Old Rugged Cross" the way she had taught her.

"On a hill far away. . ."

The girl's alto began a bit shakily, but her voice steadily gained assurance, until by the refrain, it was almost as strong as April's.

"Yes, I'll cling to the old rugged cross, And exchange it some day for a crown."

There was no doubt that the congregation enjoyed and appreciated their song, and many people told Toni so after the service ended.

"I'd sure like to have you in the choir as a regular, Toni," Ted Brown said as he took them back to April's apartment.

"So would I," April replied, but her heart ached with the knowledge that it might never come to pass.

At April's apartment they changed clothes, packed a picnic lunch and filled their water bottles, then walked their bikes to the street.

"Where are we going today?" Toni asked.

"I thought we might ride up on Warren Mountain. I'll show you the place where we had the sunrise service."

"Cool," said Toni, who would have been at the service if the Potters had been willing to take her there.

That they would have to ride past Jeremy Winter's house had nothing to do with her choice, April tried to tell herself, but her heart knew better.

ten

Jeremy had not given any thought to what his house looked like when he had brought April there on the spur of the moment, but with Joan Bell, it was different. After he got home, Jeremy changed into jeans and a sweat shirt, and he had barely finished some intensive cleaning and straightening when Joan's red sedan pulled into the driveway.

Jeremy went out to greet her. "Right on time, I see," he said.

"It's a habit with us schoolmarms," Joan said.

Jeremy smiled. As with everything else he had seen Joan wear, her jeans fit perfectly, neither tight nor baggy. She wore a blue turtleneck tee shirt over which she had layered a cotton denim shirt. "You don't look much like a schoolmarm in those jeans."

"Good. I'll be glad when I can leave that occupation."

Jeremy decided it was better not to ask Joan what occupation she might prefer to teaching. "Would you like to come inside for a minute before we start hiking?" he asked instead.

"Oh, yes. I've been dying to see what you've done with the house," Joan said, so quickly that Jeremy realized that that had probably been her main motive in coming over.

"I'm afraid you'll be disappointed. I intend to paint inside and out, but I haven't had the time."

They entered the house through the kitchen doorway, and Joan stopped and looked around thoughtfully. "This room cries out for wallpaper. It'd look really great with a chair rail and paper above it."

"I'm afraid wallpapering is out of my league," Jeremy said.

"Not mine. I'll be glad to help you if you like."

"Thanks. I'll keep that in mind."

As they walked through the other downstairs rooms, Joan had suggestions for improving each. The faded draperies in the dining room could be replaced by wooden shutters; the original wide-planked floors in the living room ought to be refinished and left uncovered; the dark hallway should be painted white.

"Are you taking notes?" Joan asked.

Jeremy knew he must look as overwhelmed as he felt, and smiled ruefully. "I doubt if I have that much paper in the house," he said.

Joan laughed "Don't worry. I'll remember every detail. Shall we go now?"

"Yes, let's, before you find anything else to do to the house."

&

The afternoon sun felt pleasantly warm on their faces as they walked up the road to a trail that Jeremy remembered from his childhood.

"It leads to the spring where Grandmother said her parents always got their water," he said.

"I'll be thirsty by the time we get there," Joan said after they had climbed almost vertically for a few minutes.

Eventually they heard the splash of water hitting rocks, and near the top of the ridge they saw the spring, issuing like a miniature waterfall from a cleft in the rocks.

"Beautiful!" Joan exclaimed. Cupping her hands, she leaned forward and drank deeply.

"Cold, too," Jeremy commented when she stepped aside to allow him to drink.

"Let's find a sunny place and sit down," Joan suggested.

"I thought you wanted to hike," Jeremy said. "We've just gotten started."

"This isn't an endurance contest," she reminded him. "Look, I see a nice, flat rock over there."

Something sunning on the rock scampered away into the underbrush at their approach, and Joan shrieked and grabbed Jeremy's arm. "I hope that wasn't a snake. I don't like snakes," she said anxiously.

"No, it was just a little lizard. I used to try to catch them, but I was never quite quick enough."

Joan nodded in agreement. "I know. A trap is the only way you can catch really fast things like that," she said.

Like men, Jeremy thought. *Women often attempt to trap a man if chasing him doesn't work.* But of course, that had nothing to do with him and Joan.

By now, Jeremy was fairly certain that he would not have to run very fast to catch Joan and if he didn't make the move himself, she just might find some way to trap him.

"Trapping sounds rather cruel," Jeremy said.

"But sometimes it's necessary," Joan said, and the way she looked at him made Jeremy know that she was not really talking about wild animals.

Did she move, or did I? Jeremy wondered. Suddenly, he felt surrounded by her presence, enveloped in her scent, so close to her that he could almost feel her breath on his cheek.

"Oh, Jeremy, you don't know what you need," Joan said. Her arms circled his neck, her head found his shoulder, and she sighed softly.

She expects me to kiss her now, Jeremy thought. *And if I don't, she'll probably kiss me.*

Joan Bell had already shown that she was not shy about

taking the lead in such matters, but for the time being, she seemed content merely to be close to Jeremy and let him make the first move.

She's going to have a long wait, Jeremy told himself.

&

"I'm out of water and I'm thirsty," Toni said halfway down Warren Mountain. "Do you have any to spare?"

April held up her water bottle to show that it, too, was empty. "No. We're near a spring that has the best water you ever tasted, but the trail is almost straight up, so we'll have to walk in."

"Suits me," Toni said.

They pedaled the short distance to the trail's start, then left their bikes in the underbrush, out of sight of anyone passing on the road.

"You weren't kidding when you said this was a steep trail," Toni said a few minutes later. Both she and April were hot and panting from their exertion by the time they reached the spring. April let Toni fill her bottle first, then filled her own and drank deeply.

"What's up there?" Toni asked, pointing to the crest of the hill.

"There's not much of a view, but it's a good place to rest."

"Let's check it out, then," said Toni.

April took the lead on the narrow path, but at the crest of the hill she stopped so suddenly that Toni ran into her. Then Toni saw what had made April stop. "Oh!" she exclaimed.

Oh, indeed! thought April. Perhaps she had suggested going up Warren Mountain in the hope of seeing Jeremy Winter, but she certainly had not expected to find him holding Joan Bell in his arms.

The instant that Jeremy realized they were not alone, he

stood, causing Joan to lose her balance and topple over on her side. Toni's first impulse was to laugh, but April's face told her she did not find anything funny about the situation.

"Excuse us," April said, at the same time that a surprised Jeremy spoke her name.

"April. . .and Toni. I didn't expect to see you two today."

"No doubt," April said coolly.

"Uh. . .you know Joan Bell, I believe? Joan, this is Toni Schmidt."

Having recovered both her balance and her poise, Joan nodded at Toni. "How do you do? I've heard that Jeremy is defending you."

"Representing, not defending," Jeremy corrected. "Toni isn't a criminal."

The girl laughed shortly. "That's not what most people in Rockdale think," she said.

"How nice that you have a good friend like April," Joan said.

"She's gonna be my guardian, too, right, Mr. Winter?"

Jeremy looked at April, but she did not return his glance. "That remains to be seen," he said.

"The hearing's coming up soon, isn't it?" Joan asked. "I'm sure you'll all be glad to have this thing settled."

"Let's go, Toni," April said.

"We just came up here for some water," Toni volunteered. "Sorry if we bothered y'all."

"No bother at all," said Joan.

❧

April's face still felt warm when she and Toni reached her apartment. With shame she admitted that she had begun to trust Jeremy enough to allow herself to admit that she cared for him. Coming upon him with Joan Bell had been like a slap in her face.

Or maybe it's a wake-up call, April told herself. At any

rate, she had no time to think about Jeremy Winter. For now, April had to find a way to tell Toni that she could not be her guardian, after all.

Dear Lord, give me the strength to do this, and give Toni the grace to accept it, she prayed.

Even so, April knew that the next few days would not be easy for either of them.

ᕒᕐ

The moment that Joan Bell looked up from Jeremy's shoulder and saw April Kincaid, she realized two things: April seemed to have some sort of romantic feelings for Jeremy and, even worse, he seemed to return them. At any rate, whatever mood Joan had managed to create between herself and Jeremy that afternoon had been totally destroyed when April and that wild Schmidt girl appeared on the scene.

"I suppose we should be getting back," Joan said when the intruders departed. Jeremy made no protest, and he said little else as they made their way back to his house. Once there, he did not suggest that Joan should come back inside.

"I'm sorry our hike was cut short," he said.

"So am I," Joan said sincerely. "We must finish it soon. Perhaps after this hearing and your business in Montgomery, we'll have more time."

"You know about Montgomery?" Jeremy asked.

Joan's laugh hinted that she knew many things of which he was unaware. "Daddy told me all about it." Her smile faded, and she adopted a serious tone as she spoke again. "He said something else, but I didn't believe it until this afternoon."

"Oh? What's that?" Jeremy asked.

"It was about April Kincaid. For your own sake, I hope you won't keep on seeing her after the hearing."

Jeremy made no effort to hide his surprise. "Your father told you I was going out with April?"

"You are, aren't you? No, don't answer. I won't make you lie. Goodbye, Jeremy. I'll see you around."

In a single fluid motion, Joan opened her car door and slid into the driver's seat. With a final wave, she turned the car around and drove away.

In near despair, Jeremy watched her go. He knew Joan had wanted him to reassure her that he cared nothing for April, but he had not been able to bring himself to do so. Even worse, the way April had looked at him when she saw him and Joan together made Jeremy know that whatever feelings she might have developed for him had probably been badly damaged, if not completely destroyed.

Furthermore, April obviously had not yet told Toni that she would not ask to be her guardian. *Maybe that's because she still wants to try for it,* Jeremy thought.

"What a mess," he said aloud, then sighed and turned and went back into his unpainted, unwallpapered, and suddenly quite empty house.

❧

Jeremy's desire for a meal he did not have to cook himself was not the only thing that sent him to Statum's Family Restaurant on Monday evening. He wanted to see April again, to try to smooth over the awkward scene that had resulted when she and Toni had found him and Joan Bell in each other's arms.

He went deliberately late, only a few minutes before Tom Statum would turn the "Open" sign to "Closed," and he sat in the booth that he had already come to think as his.

April was obviously uneasy, but when Jeremy asked to take her home, she did not refuse.

Only April's clasped hands betrayed her tension when, in her small living room, Jeremy began to try to speak something of what was on his heart.

"I've given some thought to what I said about your not asking to be Toni's guardian," he said. "Since you haven't already told her, it might be best to go on and try for it. Judge Oliver can certainly see your sincerity."

For a moment, April's cheeks grew pink as conflicting emotions played across face. Then she lowered her eyes and shook her head. "I doubt that. Anyway, it's too late. I've already told Toni."

April's expression told Jeremy what he had already guessed—that Toni had not taken the news well. "I'm sorry. I shouldn't have tried to tell you what to do."

"No, I'm glad you did. There are some things that are better left alone."

Guessing that April must be referring to her past, Jeremy leaned forward and spoke earnestly. "Would you like to tell me about it? Maybe I can help."

April shook her head. "You're Toni's lawyer, not mine," she said.

Jeremy rose and knelt before April. "I'm not here as your lawyer," he said.

April looked at him levelly. "We both know that you shouldn't have anything to do with me. You're Toni's lawyer, and I'm her friend. Let's just leave it that way, okay?"

Jeremy took both of April's hands in his and pressed them as he spoke. "I know nothing of the sort, April. You—"

April jerked her hands from his and stood. "Don't say anything else," she pleaded. "Just do your best for Toni, and leave me alone."

"I mean you no harm," Jeremy began, but April was already holding the door open, and the set of her mouth told him that further pleading would be useless. "You know where to find me if you should change your mind," Jeremy said.

"I won't," she murmured, and firmly closed the door after him.

Jeremy barely resisted the impulse to kick his front tire as he got back into the car. *I really blew it this time,* he told himself.

But he would not give up. After Toni's hearing, perhaps April would be willing to give him another chance.

❧

The insistent ringing of the telephone interrupted a dream in which Jeremy was attempting to make his first speech on the House floor, but no one seemed to be there except Guy Pettibone and Joan and Randall Bell.

With his eyes still shut, Jeremy groped for the telephone on his bedside table, spoke first into the wrong end, then reversed the receiver, tried again, and heard a voice he did not recognize.

"Mr. Winter? I'm sorry to bother you at this hour, but I thought you should know that Toni Schmidt is missing."

Jeremy opened his eyes wide and sat up in bed. "Who is this?" he asked.

"I'm sorry. I suppose I thought you'd know. This is Evelyn Trent. The Potters called me about midnight to say that Toni had apparently left the house after putting their younger children to bed. We both thought she might be at April Kincaid's apartment, so I went there first, but April says she hasn't seen Toni since Sunday night."

Jeremy squinted at his clock radio and saw it was just after two o'clock on what must be Tuesday morning—and Toni's hearing was scheduled for Wednesday. "Who else knows about this?" he asked.

"No one yet, but the Potters want to call the police. Toni rode her mountain bike home on Sunday and it's gone.

They're afraid something might have happened to Toni on her way to April's."

"I'll call the police now. Thanks for calling, Mrs. Trent. I'm sure you'd like to get some sleep now."

"As a matter of fact, I would," she replied. She hesitated for a moment, then added, "Toni has her faults, but I don't want to see anything happen to her."

"Neither do I," Jeremy said. As he replaced the receiver and climbed out of bed, he realized that the crusty appearing social worker probably felt far more emotion than she admitted, even to herself.

She might turn out to be Toni's friend, after all, he thought. But for now, his thoughts centered on someone who would need a friend of her own about now. After calling the police, Jeremy put on jeans and a well-worn college pullover that Mr. Pettibone's wardrobe specialist would never approve of, and which might even cause Joan Bell to lift an eyebrow. But Jeremy figured that April would not even notice what he wore.

She must be frantic, Jeremy thought, driving faster than usual through Rockdale's deserted streets. However, when Jeremy reached April's apartment and saw no light showing, he felt a prickle of apprehension.

Surely she didn't go out on her own to look for Toni, Jeremy told himself, but when his repeated knocking at the door brought no response, he felt real fear.

"Dear God, don't let anything happen to her," Jeremy said aloud, scarcely aware that, for the first time in a long while, he was praying.

❧

Even before April told Toni, she feared how Toni might react when she learned that April was not going to ask to be appointed her guardian. April knew Toni was in for a rough time, but after they prayed together about it, April thought that Toni had accepted the situation, although grudgingly.

However, the instant Roger Potter and Evelyn Trent appeared at her door at one o'clock on Tuesday morning, April knew she had misjudged the situation.

"We hoped to find Toni here," Mr. Potter said after telling April that the girl had been missing for several hours.

"I wish you had, but I don't know where she is, either."

"She's apparently on her bike. Where else would Toni go besides your place?"

April shook her head. "I don't know."

"Well, if she should turn up—"

"I know what to do," April finished for him. Once before, not long after Toni went to live with the Potters, she had made April an unplanned visit, and April had promptly returned the girl.

After Mr. Potter and Mrs. Trent left, April dressed and went to the corner phone booth. She had enough change to make only one call, and although April wanted to call Jeremy Winter, she did not. Mr. Potter had mentioned that Evelyn Trent was going to contact Toni's lawyer, and April did not want Jeremy to feel that he was beholden to her for anything. Besides, he was powerless to provide the kind of help she needed at a time like this.

April dropped her coins into the slot and dialed the number she had first called months before. *Don't let him have his answering machine on,* April prayed, and after four rings she was rewarded when a familiar, although sleepy, voice answered.

"Yes?"

"Pastor Hurley, this is April Kincaid. Toni's gone off somewhere, and I don't know what to do."

"Will you be at your apartment?" he asked.

"Yes."

"Keep the door locked. I'll be there as soon as I can."

Thank You, Lord, April murmured as she left the phone booth. In a crisis, there was no one she trusted more than Pastor Hurley. She would not have come to Rockdale if it had not been for him, and she certainly could not have stayed here without his continuing help.

His and the Lord's, April amended. She knew she owed them both more than she could ever repay.

But now April was not asking for help for herself, but for Toni. *Lord, just as You let Pastor Hurley help me, so let us both help her now.*

Back at her apartment, April looked up some of her favorite Scriptures, the ones that had seen her through much turmoil. It was not the first time April had faced a crisis, nor, she knew, would it be the last. But now, at least, she knew, as the hymn she often sang said, in whom she believed. And she was persuaded that He was able to keep her and guide her, and that all things would indeed work together for good in her life. But waiting for them to do so was not always easy, especially when she often felt so alone.

If only Jeremy Winter. . .

April did not let herself finish the thought. What could she have possibly hoped for from Jeremy, whose background was so different from hers, and whose plans obviously could never include her?

I was wrong to let myself hope that we could ever have a future together, April thought. Nothing could change the record of what she had once been, and it seemed that her past sins would always find her out. What April had done to herself then was bad enough; she could not let what she had been hurt anyone else.

By the time Pastor Hurley rapped on her door, April knew that her time in Rockdale, as precious as it had been, had come to an end.

eleven

Tuesday was one of the longest and most difficult days that Jeremy Winter had ever faced. From the time Evelyn Trent's phone call awakened him at two that morning, Jeremy dealt with one frustration after another.

Not only had Toni Schmidt disappeared, but no one seemed to know what had happened to April Kincaid, either. Early speculation that they were together faded when the police found that April's bike was still in her apartment, along with what seemed to be most of her clothes.

Tom Statum was equally mystified. On Tuesday morning, he had found a scrawled note on the restaurant's back door saying that April would not be at work for a while.

The police took the note and spent several hours dusting April's apartment for fingerprints, giving rise to all sorts of rumors that something might have happened to her.

"Have you contacted Judge Oliver yet?" Randall Bell asked Jeremy when they went out for lunch at a nearby cafe.

"About what?" Jeremy asked, at first not realizing what his partner was talking about. In his concern for Toni and April, he had temporarily forgotten everything else.

"The Schmidt hearing, of course," Randall Bell said. "It occurs to me that April Kincaid's mysterious disappearance and the girl's running away must have had something to do with their not wanting to appear before the judge."

"April wasn't going to petition to be Toni's guardian, and that could be why Toni ran away. Toni certainly didn't want to stay with the Potters. But April didn't know that Toni was gone until Mr. Potter and Evelyn Trent told her."

Randall Bell raised his eyebrows. "As late as Sunday afternoon, Joan heard Toni say that she was going to live with April. What makes you think that April didn't plan for the two of them to run off somewhere together?"

"For one thing, it's not like April to be underhanded. It's my guess that Toni decided to leave when she found out that April wasn't going to ask to be her guardian."

"Then where is April?"

"Looking for Toni, I suppose," Jeremy said, but even he was beginning to have his doubts, especially when the police said April's bike was still there and no one else had seen her all day.

But late that afternoon, Edith returned from the post office with the news that the police had received a call from April Kincaid.

"You have good connections with the police department," Jeremy said. "See what else you can find out about it."

The secretary hesitated for a moment. "The hearing's already been called off. What difference does it make where they are?"

"What makes you think they're together?" Jeremy asked, annoyed at Edith's lack of concern.

"Birds of a feather," she said laconically. "I'll call the Chief," she added, seeing that Jeremy had not liked her remark.

A few minutes later she returned to say that April had told the police that she was all right and urged them to concentrate on finding Toni Schmidt.

"I don't suppose they traced the call, did they?" Jeremy asked.

"Not likely, but they seem to think that April was nearby. At least they said it didn't sound like a long distance call."

"As if they'd know the difference," Jeremy muttered under his breath. "Thanks, Edith. I think I'll go now. When Mr. Bell gets back from the courthouse, tell him I'll see him tomorrow."

"May I ask where you're going?" Edith asked.

It's none of your business, Jeremy wanted to say, but he made an effort to be polite. "It's been a long day. I'm tired, and I'm going home."

"Yes, I'm sure that's a good idea," Edith said approvingly. "Shall I forward your calls?"

"Only if they concern Toni or April," he said.

❧

Jeremy had just changed into his jeans when the telephone rang. Hoping to hear that Toni had been found, he answered eagerly.

"Mr. Winter? This is Ed Hurley. Can you come to my house this evening?"

Ed Hurley? At first, Jeremy's mind drew a blank, but then Jeremy recognized the minister's distinct voice.

"What is this about?" Jeremy asked.

"Several things. I know you must be concerned about both Toni Schmidt and April."

A surge of hope quickened Jeremy's pulse. "Do you know where they are?"

"We'll discuss that when you get here. Do you know where I live?"

Jeremy took down the address. "I'll be right over," he said.

Pastor Hurley must know something, Jeremy told himself. *Let it lead me to April,* he added as he grabbed his keys and left.

❧

"Come in," Mrs. Hurley invited, opening the door of the modest frame house even before Jeremy could knock. "I just made some lemonade. Would you like some?"

"No, thanks." Jeremy looked over her shoulder and saw her husband enter the living room, alone.

The men shook hands, then Mrs. Hurley excused herself and left them alone.

"Sit down, Jeremy. I hope you don't mind if I call you that. I'm so used to hearing April speak of you that way."

"April talks about me?" Jeremy asked, surprised.

Pastor Hurley smiled briefly. "Oh, yes. . .among other things."

"Do you know where April is?" Jeremy's tone made it a question.

"I can't tell you that, but she's all right."

"What do you mean, you can't tell me?" Jeremy's concern made his tone harsh, but the pastor did not seem to notice.

"April asked me not to tell anyone where she is, but she wants you to know that she's safe."

"What about Toni?"

Pastor Hurley shook his head. "I'm sorry to say that I don't know anything about her. I'm sure that this wasn't the best time for her to take off."

Jeremy laughed without humor. "That's for sure. Judge Oliver reset the hearing for next week. If Toni isn't there, he'll issue a bench warrant for her. When she's found, she could be sent to the state school for girls without any further delay."

Pastor Hurley looked shocked. "But Toni's hardly more than a child! April was doing her so much good. I can't believe that the law would be so hard on her."

"That's the way it is, though. And that's why it's so important for us to find Toni."

Ed Hurley nodded. "Yes, April is quite aware of that."

Jeremy looked closely at the minister. "Pastor Hurley, I know April must be looking for Toni and that you're probably helping her. I don't blame you for that. But as her friend, I really care what happens to Toni, and I want to help April find her."

The minister put his hand on Jeremy's shoulder for a moment. "You care about April, as well, perhaps more than you realize. You must have patience and know that God is at work, even in this."

Jeremy shook his head. "That's hard to believe," he said.

"Yes, in the midst of a storm it's hard to imagine that the sun can ever shine again, but it's there all the time."

"And this will pass away, also," Jeremy said, his tone more bitter than accepting, as he stood to leave.

"As a matter of fact, it will, perhaps even sooner than you expect."

Jeremy went to the door, then turned back. "I'd like to know any news from either April or Toni," he said.

"Of course. And don't look so worried, Jeremy. Things are rarely as bad as we convince ourselves they're going to be."

That's easy for him to say, Jeremy thought on his way to his car. *He's not in love with April—*

Overwhelmed by what he had just admitted to himself, Jeremy almost stopped in his tracks. As unlikely, inconvenient, and inappropriate as it might be, Jeremy's feelings for April had grown so strong that now nothing else seemed more important than finding her and telling her so. On his own, however, he was not getting anywhere at all.

All right, God, help me find April, and we've got a deal.

Just what sort of deal, Jeremy did not take time to spell out; in any contract, there had to be a basic agreement before the details could be worked out.

He was willing to start from where he was, as long as the path he traveled led him to April.

❧

Dusk had yielded to darkness when Jeremy returned home, and his headlights disclosed a car in his driveway. Not just a car, but Joan Bell's sporty sedan.

"That's all I need," Jeremy muttered. He had neither seen nor talked to Joan since their somewhat awk-ward parting on Sunday. He knew that at some point they would meet again, but he had not expected it to be this soon.

Jeremy got out of his car, expecting Joan to be waiting for him in her sedan. The car was empty, however, and when Jeremy looked toward the house he saw lights illuminating the kitchen.

I'm sure I locked up when I left, Jeremy told himself when he opened the back door.

Joan stood before the stove, stirring something that filled the room with a spicy aroma.

"How did you get in?" he asked accusingly.

"I'm glad to see you, too," Joan replied mildly. "Did it occur to you that you might have left the door open?"

Jeremy shook his head. "No. I remember locking it before I left. You couldn't have found it open."

Joan's laughter was warm. "You're hard to fool, Jeremy Winter. Daddy still has a key labeled 'Warren rental.' So you see, I didn't have to break in."

"I'm sorry if I sounded short," Jeremy said. "It's just that I don't usually come home to find my supper being cooked. I presume that is what you're doing here?" he added.

"Of course. Don't look so serious, Jeremy. Daddy told me that you're taking this Toni Schmidt thing pretty hard, and I thought you could use some cheering up. It also occurred to me that you might be hungry."

"I suppose I am," Jeremy said, so obviously uncheered that Joan shook her head in mock despair.

"I was going to save my good news for dessert, but since you look so down—"

"What is it? Do you know something about April or Toni?"

Joan gave Jeremy a strange look. "How odd that you should mention April first, when Toni is your client."

Jeremy felt his face warm. "In a way they're both clients, since April wanted to be Toni's guardian. Is there news about them?"

"No, but Daddy talked to some people in Montgomery today."

"Oh, that." Jeremy made no effort to disguise his disappointment.

"You don't sound very excited for someone who just might be hand-picked to replace Harrison."

"What?" Jeremy asked.

"Go wash up. When you come back we'll eat, and I'll tell you all about it," Joan said.

Joan had made pasta, heated and added some more seasonings to some bottled spaghetti sauce from Jeremy's cabinet, and made a salad from fixings she found in the refrigerator. She had brought a loaf of homemade bread and a quart of chocolate mint ice cream, both of which she knew Jeremy liked.

"Everything is good, but I'm not very hungry," he told Joan a few minutes later when she scolded him for not eating much. "I've had a lot on my mind, having to cancel Toni's hearing and. . .and everything," he finished lamely, aware that he should not mention April's name again.

Joan leaned across the table and smiled at Jeremy, and the subtle fragrance she wore wafted toward him. "Maybe the latest news from Montgomery will help restore your appetite," she said.

Jeremy pushed his chair back from the table and folded his arms across his chest, his body language unconsciously proclaiming that he was not as excited about developments in the state capital as she was. "What's happening?"

"Daddy's been on the phone with several important people. They're having a big meeting soon, and Daddy says they want you to come and see them."

It was the kind of break that Guy Pettibone and Randall Bell had both worked on to give Jeremy a once-in-a-lifetime chance to make a good impression with some of the most powerful people in the state. The ambitious part of Jeremy's mind told him he should be turning cartwheels, yet his heart still felt strangely detached from the good news.

"Any idea what 'soon' means?"

Joan sighed as if his reaction had disappointed her. "This week, I presume."

The telephone rang, and Jeremy bolted from the table to answer it, hoping to hear April's voice. Instead, it was Guy Pettibone, who repeated what Joan had just told him and added another piece of information.

"Harrison's called a press conference for Friday morning. It's presumed that he'll announce his retirement then. Get on down to Montgomery and be ready to strut your stuff, boy."

"Suppose the Governor has already decided to appoint someone as a political payback?" Jeremy asked.

"It won't matter. Whoever it is will still have to run again when the term's up, but the sooner you get some state backing, the better. You understand what I'm saying, boy? You don't sound right."

"Yes, sir, I understand," Jeremy said. "It's been a long day, and I'm just a little tired."

"Perk up and get on down to Montgomery. Call me from there."

Jeremy hung up the receiver and came back into the kitchen. When he saw Joan at the sink, it was all he could do to not tell her to go home and leave him alone. *You're a nice woman, but you're standing where April stood.* Jeremy remembered quite well how he had kissed April there, and how for one breathless moment she had returned his kiss.

Joan turned to face Jeremy. "Any news?" she asked.

"No. Look, Joan, it was great of you to make supper, and I appreciate it. But if you don't mind—"

"I know. You can't wait to get rid of me," she interrupted, "and I'll go as soon as we've done the dishes. Get a towel and start wiping. I'll wash."

Feeling guilty that he had been so cool when Joan had gone out of her way to be nice to him, Jeremy pretended to be interested as she talked about some of the people he would meet in Montgomery.

When the dishes were done and Jeremy walked Joan to her car, he even leaned over to brush her cheek with a thank-you kiss.

"You can do better than that." Joan put her hands to Jeremy's face and placed her lips on his for a long moment, leaving no doubt that his apparent lack of interest had not discouraged her.

"Joan, you should know—" Jeremy began.

"We both know all we need to know," she said enigmatically. "One of these days you'll realize what you really need."

I already have, Jeremy thought, but he let Joan get into her car and leave without telling her so.

When April came back—he would not allow himself to think she might not—he would have to tell her how he felt about her. He hoped—even prayed—that she would share his feelings.

But in any case, Jeremy knew that if his political ambitions were to be realized, he would still need Joan and her father's help. To say anything about April now would be premature, and probably even disastrous.

You're a coward, Jeremy Winter, he told himself in disgust.

But for the moment, he did not think he had any other choice.

twelve

Wednesday began little better than the day before and became even worse when police in nearby Ft. Payne found a mountain bike fitting the description of Toni Schmidt's abandoned near the bus station.

"They think she rode it there intending to take a bus out of town," Randall Bell told Jeremy shortly after noon.

"Does anybody remember seeing her?"

"Not at the bus station, but the driver of a wrecker on an accident call saw someone about Toni's size, walking along the side of the road, and guessed she was hitchhiking."

That doesn't sound at all good, Jeremy thought. However, if April were, indeed, looking for Toni, she should know about this latest development. *I'll make sure that Ed Hurley hears about it,* he decided.

Aloud, he told Mr. Bell that he was about to leave the office. "I have to deliver the Morgan mortgage papers, then I think I'll go on home."

"Why don't you come for supper tonight? I'm sure Joan won't mind, and we need to talk about strategy for Montgomery."

"Thanks, but I'm not up to it tonight."

"Then we'll expect you tomorrow night. . .unless the call comes from Montgomery before then."

Jeremy did not really look forward to seeing Joan again, but in the meantime, other things—and one certain other person—totally occupied his mind.

The Community Church parking lot contained quite a few cars when Jeremy pulled into it early that evening. He had not been to a Wednesday night church service in many years, but Pastor Hurley had urged Jeremy to come, saying that the whole congregation would like to hear the news he had about Toni Schmidt.

"That little girl kind of got next to a lot of us," Mrs. Hurley said when she saw Jeremy enter the church. "Come on down and sit with me," she added.

About half the people who attended on Sundays were present for this Wednesday service, but they made up in fervor what they lacked in number. The opening hymns, "What A Friend We Have in Jesus" and "Sweet Hour of Prayer," set the tone for the rest of the informal service, in which requests for prayer produced a number of earnest petitions.

After several people's needs had been noted and prayed for, Pastor Hurley asked Jeremy to join him at the pulpit and share what he knew about Toni Schmidt and April Kincaid with them all. When he finished and sat down, Pastor Hurley spoke again.

"We may not know where Toni is, but we know Whose she is, and we know that He shares our concern for her safety. As you are led, pray now for Toni Schmidt."

Several men and women did so before their pastor concluded with his own prayer, in which Jeremy was surprised to find himself mentioned.

"Finally, Lord, we thank You for Jeremy Winter and for the help he has been so willing to give Toni. Lead this fine young man in the paths of righteousness, and bring him to know Your perfect Will for his life. Amen."

"Amen," everyone murmured, then someone, Jeremy supposed it was Tim Brown, began "Blest Be the Tie That Binds," and the members of the congregation joined in as they hugged one another in farewell.

"May the Lord bless you and keep you," Mrs. Hurley murmured when she embraced Jeremy.

"You, too." Instead of moving toward the door with the others, Jeremy stayed behind, feeling that he had some unfinished business there. He wanted to kneel at the altar and rest his head on the polished rail as he had done as a boy. In those days his grandmother had told him that his prayers flew straight to God, and what he asked, believing, he would receive. But she had added something else—*As long as it is in God's will for you.*

Jeremy had no memory of moving to the altar, but there he was, kneeling before it, its smooth wooden rail comforting his forehead as he poured out his heart to God. For the first time, Jeremy questioned whether his political ambitions, which had always seemed so right, were really in God's Will.

I believe, Lord. Help Thou my unbelief.

With the admission came the first peace that Jeremy had known since April and Toni had disappeared. Some time later—Jeremy could not say how much longer—he heard a distinct and clear voice apparently addressing him directly.

Do not concern yourself about April and Toni. They are resting in God's care, and so should you be.

Startled, Jeremy looked over his left shoulder to see who had spoken, and saw no one. He stood, but his legs were so stiff from the unaccustomed kneeling that they almost gave way.

"Come over here and sit down," Pastor Hurley said from a pew on the right side of the church.

Jeremy wondered how long he had been watching him, but it did not really matter. "April and Toni are all right," he said when he joined the pastor.

Ed Hurley nodded. "That's not the only thing you found out here tonight, is it?"

"No," Jeremy said. He paused for a moment, struggling to put his feelings into words. "It's almost like coming home, to kneel at this altar again and feel, actually *know*, the power of something outside myself again."

"That's the joy of your salvation at work," Ed Hurley said.

"I'm not sure I understand it," Jeremy admitted. For another half-hour he and the pastor talked, then prayed, and Jeremy found himself telling Ed Hurley that his political ambitions now seemed vain and inconsequential. "What matters most to me now is finding April and Toni," he concluded.

Ed Hurley looked closely at Jeremy. "We all share concern for Toni, but I must ask. . .how do you feel about April?"

Jeremy replied without hesitation, "I love her. I can't imagine my future without her."

The pastor nodded. "I think April knew that before you did. She asked me not to tell you where she was, but now I believe I should."

"You really know where she is?" Jeremy asked.

"Yes. She borrowed Mrs. Hurley's car and went to Chattanooga to look for Toni. Earlier today she called to say that Toni wasn't at her aunt's house, but she thought she might still show up there."

"April's in Chattanooga?" Jeremy glanced at his watch. "I can get there in a couple of hours—"

"Just a minute," Pastor Hurley cautioned. "Before I tell you where to find April, there's something you should know about her."

"April never said anything about her past, but apparently she thinks she has something to hide. Is that what you mean?"

"Yes and no. Jeremy, as a lawyer, you're used to seeing things in terms of right and wrong, black and white. What April might once have done has nothing to do with the beautiful person that she is today, but she doesn't want her past to hurt your career."

"I don't care about what April might have done. . .just tell me where to find her."

Ed Hurley regarded Jeremy gravely. "In God's eyes, every saint has a past and every sinner has a future. Can you really accept that fact?"

"I already have," Jeremy assured him.

"Then I think it's time for you to tell April so."

Jeremy's first impulse was to go directly to Chattanooga without letting anyone know, but he stopped in the parking lot of a darkened business and punched the Bells' number into his cellular telephone.

"Are you all right? Daddy's been trying to reach you for hours," Joan said as soon as she heard Jeremy's voice.

"I'm fine," Jeremy said. "I have a lead that Toni Schmidt might be in Chattanooga and I'm going to follow it up. Tell your father that I'll call him tomorrow."

Joan sounded almost frantic. "You can't leave town now. Daddy talked to the Montgomery people this evening and they want to see you tomorrow."

"What time?" Jeremy asked.

"About noon, I think Daddy said."

Jeremy reviewed what he had to do and mentally calculated the driving time from Chattanooga to Huntsville and then to Montgomery. "Tell him I don't think I can make it."

Joan sounded exasperated. "Have you suddenly taken leave of your senses? This could be your big break, Jeremy. You'll need these people—"

"Look, Joan, I have to go now," Jeremy interrupted. "Just tell your father what I said."

"All right. I hope you know what you're doing."

"Oh, yes. For the first time, I really do."

❧

It was nearly midnight when Jeremy pulled into the driveway of a modest frame house in the Brainerd section of Chattanooga. He was disappointed not to see Mrs. Hurley's car in the driveway, but so many lights burned in both the upper and lower floors that Jeremy thought that Ed Hurley must have called to tell his sister that Jeremy was on his way to see April.

However, it was obvious that the man who turned on the porch light and peered out the door at Jeremy did not know who he was, and only after Jeremy explained that Pastor Hurley had given him directions to the house did the man relax his guard and open the door to him.

"Who is it now?" a female voice called out, and Jeremy saw a middle-aged woman resembling Ed Hurley join her husband.

"I'm Jeremy Winter, Mrs. Watkins. Pastor Hurley told me that April Kincaid was here."

"What do you want with April? Are you some kind of policeman?" Mr. Watkins asked.

"Oh, hush," his wife said. "This must be the young fellow that April talked about so much. If my brother told you she was here, then I'm sure it's all right."

"The thing is, she's not here now," Mr. Watkins added.

"Don't look so worried," his wife told Jeremy. "She had a call from Toni's aunt that the police were holding the girl, and she went to try to get her released."

"When did that happen?" Jeremy asked.

"About ten o'clock, I think. I told her to wait until Mr.

Watkins got home—he works second shift—but she said she could handle it herself and off she went."

"I see," said Jeremy, who could, indeed, imagine April's impatience to go to Toni. "Where is this police station?"

"I could tell you, but it'd be easier if I rode with you," Mr. Watkins said.

"Let's go, then."

Mrs. Watkins followed them to the car. "Tell April that I've made up a bed for Toni."

"God willing, we'll we back soon with both of them," Mr. Watkins said.

"How long have you known April?" Jeremy asked on the drive to police headquarters.

"Several years now, I reckon," he replied. "Mrs. Watkins met her when she was doing some mission work at a homeless shelter. She was so taken with April that she asked Ed Hurley to keep looking after her when she was ready to go out on her own."

"April lived in a homeless shelter?"

Mr. Watkins cast Jeremy a worried look. "She didn't tell you? Well, it's nothing she's proud of, I'm sure, but you have to give her credit for what she's made of her life since the bad times."

"I know," Jeremy said. "April is a wonderful person, and she's been a big help to Toni."

"You're Toni's lawyer?"

"Yes. But I also think of Toni as a friend."

"And April?"

Jeremy hesitated for a moment, then for the second time in only a few hours he repeated a truth he had only lately come to admit. "I love her."

❧

The desk sergeant did not seem to know where Toni and

April were, but another officer told them that Toni was being held for pickup by the juvenile authorities. April had tried to get Toni released to her custody, but the request had been denied.

"Where is Miss Kincaid now?" Jeremy asked.

"At the pay phone, I suppose. She said some lawyer in Alabama represented the girl, and she went to call him to come after her."

Jeremy adopted his most authoritative voice. "I'm Toni Schmidt's lawyer, and I'm here to take her back to Rockdale, where she has a court hearing pending."

Jeremy thought the officer looked almost relieved to have an excuse to be rid of her. "I'll get the paperwork started," he replied.

"Where are the pay phones?" Jeremy asked, looking around and seeing none.

"Down the hall and to the right, beside the lockers. You can use my desk phone if you like—"

But Jeremy was already gone.

❧

April stood by the graffiti-filled wall beside the pay phones, speaking in a voice that was strained, but under control. "I'm sorry to call so late, Pastor Hurley, but I've found Toni. . . Yes, praise the Lord, indeed. She's all right, just tired and scared. But the police won't let her go with me. I tried to called Jeremy Winter, but I got his answering machine. Will you keep trying to reach him and tell him—What? Are you sure?"

At the same moment that Pastor Hurley was telling April that Jeremy Winter was on his way to Chattanooga, possibly was already there, Jeremy touched her lightly on the shoulder, and April almost dropped the receiver when she turned and saw him.

Jeremy took the receiver from her hand. "Pastor? I'm here, and the police are going to release Toni to me. We'll be coming back to Rockdale tomorrow. Yes, sir, I agree. Thank you. Goodbye." He hung up and turned to April, confident that the love and joy that filled his heart must surely show in his face.

"Jeremy—" April began before he swept her into his arms and held her in a fierce embrace.

All the way to Chattanooga, Jeremy had rehearsed what he would say when he saw April. He would speak logically and tell her he did not care what might have happened in her life before they met. But now that she was in his arms at last, all other words fled except the only ones that mattered.

"I love you, April."

April pulled slightly away and looked at Jeremy, revealing the tears in her hazel eyes. "You shouldn't," she almost whispered. "I'm too far out of your league. I'd just drag you down—"

"Let me worry about that." Jeremy silenced her further protests with a long, tender kiss and felt her gradually relax in his arms. Even before she whispered the words, April's response told him how she really felt.

"God help me, I love you, too, Jeremy Winter."

Jeremy's sudden laughter startled April, and she looked at him in alarm before he hugged her close again.

"God will help us both," he corrected. "I know that now."

"I'm glad," April said simply.

When she kissed him again, Jeremy quietly acknowledged that knowing and finding God's Will for their lives would always be the most politically correct thing they could ever do.

epilogue

On the last Tuesday in August, some four months after Jeremy returned to Rockdale with Toni and April, the voters of Rockdale went to the polls to elect a number of local and state officials. Jeremy and April cast their ballots early in the day, then joined a group of Jeremy's supporters at Statum's Family Restaurant to await the outcome.

"Don't call it a victory party," Jeremy warned when Tom Statum told him about his plans for the gathering.

"Everybody in town knows that you're the best man for the job, but I'll just call it an election celebration if that's what you want."

As they entered, the number of people who had come to Statum's Family Restaurant surprised Jeremy. He had expected to see the Bells (accompanied by a man rumored to be "really serious" about Joan) and Edith Westleigh from the law office. He knew Evelyn Trent and her ward, Toni Schmidt, who had worked tirelessly for his campaign, would be there, along with the pastor, choir, and a great many members of Community Church, where Jeremy and April would exchange marriage vows in September. But he had not expected to see so many others, from the Country Club set to the residents of Harrison Homes, that filled every table in the small restaurant and stood along the wall or sat on the floor.

Jeremy's entrance brought a cheer from the crowd to which he waved in reply.

"Get ready to make a speech when the results come in,"

Tom Statum said, as if he had been managing political campaigns all his life.

Jeremy and April took their reserved places at the counter, from which Tom was dispensing more of the free lemonade that had been the main symbol in Jeremy's campaign.

"When life hands you a lemon, you'd better learn how to make lemonade," was a slogan that Jeremy had borrowed from April, who in turn had heard it from some anonymous worker at the homeless shelter in the darkest days of her life.

When the people in Montgomery decided to appoint Mrs. Harrison to fill out her husband's unexpired term, Jeremy had not wasted any time feeling sorry for himself. By then, he had discovered several ways in which Rockdale could improve itself, and when Randall Bell urged him to run for mayor, Jeremy had been surprised at the support he had been given. Dallas Alston, Rockdale's longtime mayor, had been merely going through the motions for several years, and the town was ready for a change.

Jeremy ran on a platform of civic improvement, with emphasis on finding ways to keep the young people occupied and providing help for those who got into trouble, improving the police department, and attracting the right kind of new business to insure an adequate tax base to pay for it all. Among those who had become interested in his campaign was the millionaire Jackie Tyler, who had never before participated in Rockdale's civic life. He financed a barbecue at which a number of his well-known musician friends performed a catchy campaign song featuring the words, "Win with Winter."

"Wait until Mr. Pettibone hears this," Jeremy told April, who looked at him questioningly.

"I thought you fired him."

"I tried to, but he still wants me to run for Harrison's seat when his widow gives it up."

"Even though you'll have a wife with a juvenile record?"

"I explained that you ran away from a bad family situation and got in with the wrong crowd for a while, and Mr. Pettibone said that as long as we were up front about it, no harm would be done. In fact, he admires the way you've overcome your past." Jeremy paused, seeing the doubt in April's face. "But that's still a long time off, and in the meantime if I win this election, I'll have all the politics I can handle right here in Rockdale."

"With them fancy electronic machines they use now, it seems to me that they should be done with the counting by now," Tom Statum said a few minutes after Jeremy and April's arrival.

Just then the telephone rang, and the noisy babble of dozens of conversations stopped as he picked up the receiver and listened for a moment. Then Tom's face broke into a wide grin, and everyone cheered the results they knew he must have heard.

Tom hung up the telephone and pounded Jeremy on the back. "Congratulations, Mr. Mayor. You won in a landslide!"

After a few minutes of applauding and cheering, the crowd silenced when Jeremy stood to speak to them.

"Thank you all for being here and for your support these past few months. Most of you know I decided to run for mayor when I realized how few opportunities Rockdale has for young people, and after the folks at Community Church and First Church urged me to get involved. With your hard work and the help of the Lord, we all won today. You know I'll be new at this, and April and I will need your continued support, as well as all your prayers, to serve all the people of Rockdale. Thank you again, and praise God!"

When he sat down, Jeremy noticed that April's eyes were damp with tears of joy.

"I have so much to be thankful for, starting with you," she said softly, as if they were the only people there.

Jeremy squeezed her hand. "We both do," he replied.

Their brief private moment was interrupted by a number of well-wishers.

"Nice job, Mr. Mayor," Joan Bell said sincerely. Once she had finally accepted the fact that Jeremy really intended to marry April Kincaid, Joan had become a staunch friend of them both.

Jeremy nodded. "Thanks. I know I wouldn't even have run for mayor if you and your father hadn't pushed so hard."

"Remember, we'll still be around for your next race."

After Joan, Jackie Tyler offered his hand. "Congratulations, Jeremy." Then he turned to April and spoke with sincere admiration. "My offer still stands, young lady. I'm about to produce a new album and I sure could use a voice like yours to sing backup."

"I'll keep your offer in mind," April said, but her tone left no doubt that she would not be likely to take him up on it.

Mr. Tyler grinned and slapped Jeremy on the back. "I hope you know how lucky you are," he said.

"Blessed, not lucky," Jeremy corrected.

It's true, Jeremy thought as he spoke the words. No matter what lay ahead, Jeremy felt certain that the firm and sure hand of the Lord would continue to be in control of his life.

As if she knew and shared his thoughts, April squeezed his hand.

For now, Jeremy Winter would try to be the best mayor Rockdale ever had. If God had another political job for him to do later on down the road, then so be it.

Jeremy and April would be ready.

A Letter To Our Readers

Dear Reader:

In order that we might better contribute to your reading enjoyment, we would appreciate your taking a few minutes to respond to the following questions. When completed, please return to the following:

Rebecca Germany, Managing Editor
Heartsong Presents
P.O. Box 719
Uhrichsville, Ohio 44683

1. Did you enjoy reading *Politically Correct*?
   ❏ Very much. I would like to see more books
      by this author!
   ❏ Moderately
      I would have enjoyed it more if _____

   _____

2. Are you a member of **Heartsong Presents**? ❏Yes ❏No
   If no, where did you purchase this book? _____

   _____

3. What influenced your decision to purchase this
   book? (Check those that apply.)

   ❏ Cover   ❏ Back cover copy

   ❏ Title   ❏ Friends

   ❏ Publicity   ❏ Other_____

4. How would you rate, on a scale from 1 (poor) to 5
   (superior), the cover design? _____

5. On a scale from 1 (poor) to 10 (superior), please rate the following elements.

___Heroine   ___Plot

___Hero   ___Inspirational theme

___Setting   ___Secondary characters

6. What settings would you like to see covered in **Heartsong Presents** books?_____

_____

_____

7. What are some inspirational themes you would like to see treated in future books?_____

_____

_____

8. Would you be interested in reading other **Heartsong Presents** titles?   ❏ Yes   ❏ No

9. Please check your age range:
   ❏ Under 18   ❏ 18-24   ❏ 25-34
   ❏ 35-45   ❏ 46-55   ❏ Over 55

10. How many hours per week do you read? _____

Name _____

Occupation _____

Address _____

City_____ State_____ Zip_____

Romance is Back
"Inn" Style!

From New England to Hawaii and Canada to the Caribbean, *The Christian Bed & Breakfast Directory* has a romantic home-away-from-home waiting for your pleasure. The 1997-98 edition of the directory includes over 1,400 inns. Choose from secluded cabins, beachfront bungalows, historical mansion suites, and much more.

Relevant information about bed and breakfast establishments and country inns is included, inns that are eager to host Christian travelers like you. You'll find descriptions of the inns and accommodation details, telephone numbers and rates, credit card information, and surrounding attractions that satisfy a variety of interests and ages. Maps are also included to help you plan a wonderful romantic getaway.

608 pages; paperbound; 5" x 8"

········ Presents ········

__HP134 THE ROAD HOME, *Susannah Hayden*
__HP137 DISTANT LOVE, *Ann Bell*
__HP138 ABIDING LOVE, *Elizabeth Murphy*
__HP142 FLYING HIGH, *Phyllis A. Humphrey*
__HP145 MOCKING BIRD'S SONG, *Janet Gortsema*
__HP146 DANCING IN THE DARKNESS, *Janelle Burnham*
__HP149 LLAMA LAND, *VeraLee Wiggins*
__HP150 TENDER MERCY, *Elizabeth Murphy*
__HP153 HEALING LOVE, *Ann Bell*
__HP154 CALLIE'S CHALLENGE, *Veda Boyd Jones*
__HP157 POCKETFUL OF PROMISES, *Loree Lough*
__HP158 ON WINGS OF SONG, *Brenda Knight Graham*
__HP161 MONTANA SKY, *Loree Lough*
__HP162 GOLDEN DREAMS, *Kathleen Yapp*
__HP165 CONSIDER HER WAYS, *Fran Vincent*
__HP166 A GIFT FROM ABOVE, *Dina Leonhardt Koehly*
__HP169 GARMENT OF PRAISE, *Becky Melby and Cathy Wienke*
__HP170 AGAINST THAT DAY, *Rae Simons*
__HP173 THE HASTY HEART, *Helen Spears*

__HP174 BEHIND THE SCENES, *Gloria Brandt*
__HP177 NEPALI NOON, *Susannah Hayden*
__HP178 EAGLES FOR ANNA, *Cathrine Runyon*
__HP181 RETREAT TO LOVE, *Nancy N. Rue*
__HP182 A WING AND A PRAYER, *Tracie J. Peterson*
__HP185 ABIDE WITH ME, *Una McManus*
__HP186 WINGS LIKE EAGLES, *Tracie J. Peterson*
__HP189 A KINDLED SPARK, *Colleen L. Reece*
__HP190 A MATTER OF FAITH, *Nina Coombs Pykare*
__HP193 COMPASSIONATE LOVE, *Ann Bell*
__HP194 WAIT FOR THE MORNING, *Kjersti Hoff Baez*
__HP197 EAGLE PILOT, *Jill Stengl*
__HP198 WATERCOLOR CASTLES, *Ranee McCollum*
__HP201 A WHOLE NEW WORLD, *Yvonne Lehman*
__HP202 SEARCH FOR TODAY, *Mary Hawkins*
__HP205 A QUESTION OF BALANCE, *Veda Boyd Jones*
_·HP206 POLITICALLY CORRECT, *Kay Cornelius*

Great Inspirational Romance at a Great Price!

Heartsong Presents books are inspirational romances in contemporary and historical settings, designed to give you an enjoyable, spiritlifting reading experience. You can choose wonderfully written titles from some of today's best authors like Veda Boyd Jones, Yvonne Lehman, Tracie J. Peterson, Nancy N. Rue, and many others.

When ordering quantities less than twelve, above titles are $2.95 each.

SEND TO: Heartsong Presents Reader's Service
P.O. Box 719, Uhrichsville, Ohio 44683

Please send me the items checked above. I am enclosing $_____
(please add $1.00 to cover postage per order. OH add 6.25% tax. NJ add 6%.). Send check or money order, no cash or C.O.D.s, please.
To place a credit card order, call 1-800-847-8270.

NAME _____

ADDRESS _____

CITY/STATE_____ ZIP _____

HPS 1-97

Heartsong Presents
Love Stories Are Rated G!

That's for godly, gratifying, and of course, great! If you love a thrilling love story, but don't appreciate the sordidness of some popular paperback romances, **Heartsong Presents** is for you. In fact, **Heartsong Presents** is the *only inspirational romance book club*, the only one featuring love stories where Christian faith is the primary ingredient in a marriage relationship.

Sign up today to receive your first set of four, never before published Christian romances. Send no money now; you will receive a bill with the first shipment. You may cancel at any time without obligation, and if you aren't completely satisfied with any selection, you may return the books for an immediate refund!

Imagine. . .four new romances every four weeks—two historical, two contemporary—with men and women like you who long to meet the one God has chosen as the love of their lives. . .all for the low price of $9.97 postpaid.

To join, simply complete the coupon below and mail to the address provided. **Heartsong Presents** romances are rated G for another reason: They'll arrive *Godspeed!*